CORKTOWN

Ty Hutchinson

This book is a work of fiction. Names, characters, places, and incidents are the product of the author's imagination or are used fictitiously. Any resemblance to actual events, locales, or persons, living or dead, is coincidental.

All rights reserved. No part of this book may be reproduced, stored in a retrieval system, transmitted in any form or by any means, electronic, mechanical, photocopying, recording, or otherwise, without the prior written permission of the author, Ty Hutchinson.

Gangkruptcy Press, San Francisco, CA
Copyright © 2012 by Ty Hutchinson
Cover Design: Kay Hutchison
Right House Photo: Detroiturbex.com
Middle House Photo: Kevin Bauman
100abandonedhouses.com
Left House Photo: Brandon Bartoszek
Dead Guy Photo: Dave & Les Jacobs (Getty Images)
Back Cover Photo: DetroitDerek Photograph (Derek Farr)

Thank You

A lot of people helped me with this book. I'd like to let them know that I appreciate them. A big thanks to my beta readers: Erica Kim, Ethan Jones, Ke'ala Pasco and Sharon Hutchinson. I'd like to give a special thanks to my editor, Kristen King. I know it seemed like the writing of this book went on forever. I'd also like to thank my proofreader, Ashley Case. Lastly, I want to give a big thanks to my FBI source, a long time friend of the family. You know who you are. You helped me turn Abby Kane into Agent Abby Kane. Okay, cue the music and kick me off the stage.

For my wife, Mila

CORKTOWN

1

To be honest, I never had many girlfriends growing up. They seemed to come and go. As a teen, I was a bit of a tomboy. I preferred hunting trips with my father to hair braiding sleepovers with girls from school. I liked boys, but second dates were hard to come by after my suitors met my father: the tall, broad-shouldered Irishman that hovered behind me. In lieu of dating, my father taught me to bare-knuckle fight, a favorite pastime in Ireland, he would say. When I graduated from Hong Kong's Police College at age nineteen, unheard of for a woman, he told me, "I'm proud of you, son."

I like to think he was joking.

From that point on, my career in law enforcement became my focus; it took over my life. It left little time for what few friends I had and completely ruined any chance of a romance with someone other than myself. My relationships were pathetic at best and upsetting for my mother. All she had ever wanted were grandchildren. *What about me, the child you birthed?*

"Why, Abby?" she would start over Sunday dinner. "Why are you not married? What is wrong? Are you a lazi?"

"What?"

"I knew it; you're a lazi."

"I'm not a lazi!"

I finally proved my mother wrong eight years later when I married a man.

Peng Yee was my first true love. He also showed me there was more to life than the job. We enjoyed six months of marital bliss. I say six months because that's how long we had been married before my old partner, a good friend, sat me down and told me my husband had just been found brutally murdered.

We had no motive and no knowledge of enemies Peng might have had. I wasn't prepared for that—life shoving its hand into my chest and ripping out all that mattered.

He left me with two young children, Ryan and Lucy, and a mother-in-law, Po Po. Peng was a widower when we fell in love; now I was a widow, and a stepmother to boot.

I dealt with his death by throwing myself into my work. I had all but abandoned the family during that time. My stepchildren were strangers to me and Po Po was fast becoming their mother, a job I slowly started to realize I wanted. So I did what I thought was best. I quit the force and moved the family to San Francisco for a new start on life. Mine, mostly.

• • •

I checked my watch—ten to seven. I picked up the pace on my Sunday morning run, enough to get the endorphins flowing and the hair tangled. Po Po would already be up, puttering around the kitchen, doing the job I should have been doing—the job of mom. I turned onto Pfeiffer Street and walked four houses toward our Victorian—a fixer-upper.

As soon as I stepped inside, the smell of pancakes filled my nostrils. Po Po stood next to the kitchen counter in her blue and white nightgown making a batch of everyone's favorite, blueberry. Her arm jerked back and forth, mixing more batter than necessary. Ever since she'd discovered Bisquick, we'd been eating silver dollars quite regularly.

"Why are you cooking now?" I asked. "They won't be up for another half hour."

"You eat," she said, staring at me in her loving yet authoritative way.

It irritated me that she made the kids breakfast every morning. *Does she know that?* That should have been my job. I worked during the week and almost never got home before 5:00 p.m., when old people and small children liked to eat.

I should have been grateful to have a mother-in-law who wanted to help out. But deep down inside, I wanted to be the awesome supermom fixing her kids' meals yet still managing a career. In the meantime, I focused on mastering the not-tired-when-I-came-home-from-work role.

A month after arriving in the States, I took a job as a federal agent investigating white-collar crime, mostly fraud.

I know it made no sense for a burned out detective to join the FBI, but I needed a J.O.B.

"I'll eat after my shower," I called out to her.

I headed upstairs to my bedroom and started the shower before stripping off my running gear. With my new career, I actually had time to practice an active lifestyle. Even though I had the metabolism of a cheetah, I missed the high those double-digit runs had fueled.

I moved my finger across my stomach and traced the noticeable six-pack before clucking my lips and patting my tummy. *You still got it.* I couldn't take all the credit, though. Both of my parents passed along their best genes, except for one thing; my Chinese mother blessed me with her short stature. Despite that, I stood proud at five foot one.

My hair, however, was another matter. I longed for curvy body but settled for straight silk. I turned so my back faced the mirror. I had started to grow out my shoulder length hair; it popped nicely against my fair skin.

In the shower, my skin tingled under the delicious warmth. I had one of those rain showerheads and it felt like hundreds of fingertips tapping away on my body. Speaking of tapping, my bathroom door had opened and the tap-tap of tiny feet made their way across the floor.

"Is that you, Lucy?" She was my youngest, age five. Ryan was eight.

I heard her yawn before she answered. "Yes, Mommy."

"Didn't Mommy tell you not to come into the

bathroom when other people are using it?"

"I had to pee-pee."

"What's wrong with the hallway bathroom?"

"Ryan's hogging it."

Lucy was the only one who called me Mommy. Ryan called me Abby. It didn't bother me. I completely understood. He was old enough to remember his mother. She had died shortly after Lucy was born. As far as the five year-old was concerned, I was her mother, and I liked that.

By the time I had made my way back downstairs, both kids were eating their fluffy stacks. I poured myself a cup of tea and sat at the table, where the *San Francisco Chronicle* waited for me. I picked up a knife and fork, preparing to cut Lucy's meal, only to see someone had beaten me to it, and that someone had already read halfway through her copy of the *Sing Tao Daily*.

Before I could think of a clever remark, we all heard impatient rapping at the front door. All eyes fell upon me, so I got up and did my duty.

"Abby, sorry to disturb you so early." My unofficial partner, Agent Trey Wilkinson, stood outside my door and he didn't look too happy.

I stepped onto the front porch and closed the door behind me. "You okay?"

"Yeah, I'm fine," he said, adjusting his Oakland A's cap.

While we weren't exactly assigned partners, he and I

had worked closely together on a number of small cases. Wilkinson was a rising star inside the Bureau and was a great help to me in the beginning. We had a friendly relationship. I occasionally called him Wilky. Whenever possible, we would seek the other one out and team on a case. We respected each other's abilities.

"You remember telling me how you enjoyed your job with the FBI, how easy breezy it was?"

My right eyebrow rose, giving him my answer.

"Well, Detroit Metro Police had a couple of homicides pop up. There are similarities between the cases and the detectives think they might have a serial killer on their hands."

"Really? How many so far?"

"Two."

"Don't you need three to officially qualify or is it different in the States?"

My partner shrugged and nodded. "That's not all though; they want us to fly out today."

My gut tightened a bit. I didn't expect to hear that.

"We're to be briefed first thing Monday morning," he said as he looked down and kicked at the porch with the tip of his sneaker. "Sorry about ruining your Sunday."

I knew it wasn't his doing. He was only the messenger. I poked him. "Hey, we can enjoy each other's misery on the flight."

Wilkinson smiled again. He may have been thirty, but

he looked twenty-two.

Breaking the news to everyone wasn't something I looked forward to doing. For the last six months, we had lived as a normal family. We were happy, content and gelling. My new job allowed me the flexibility to take off for an hour so I could walk Ryan and Lucy home from school on a somewhat regular basis. I had even attended my first PTA meeting.

And now the job was getting in the way, again.

As I headed back inside, Po Po saw it on my face. She knew what a hushed conversation outside meant.

Five hours later, Wilkinson and I were sitting in coach and halfway to Detroit. I already missed Po Po and the kids. But to be honest, the chase excited me.

2

"I'm horny," she said.

"I'm driving back from Kalamazoo," he said.

"It's Sunday evening. Why aren't you home?" she cooed, allowing the last word to trail. "I need you to take care of me."

"I'm three hours away."

"Hurry."

Recently divorced, with her kids away in college, Marian Ward had started to enjoy her single life. It got better when she met Paul Poole, an engineer at Ford. He had turned Marian on to her first screaming "O," as well as a slew of other sexual firsts. He also opened her eyes to the wonderful world of BDSM. She couldn't get enough of the whipping, clamping, and toy-infused lifestyle. From the start, she was hooked.

Completely nude, except for the dangles of bling around her neck and wrists, Marian stood in front of her oak-framed, floor mirror. She twirled around, bent over and struck other seductive poses. *Not bad for a forty-six year-old.* By all accounts, the five-foot-seven brunette took the term MILF to a whole new level. Marian was extremely proud of her tight stomach and taut butt. Her early morning gym visits kept those areas in check and her social calendar full. She paid for a lift in the bosom department, but you couldn't blame her; her age and two kids made it inevitable. Plus, she had a life now.

She entered her walk-in closet and continued toward the back wall where there were four customized drawers built in. All were filled with fun stuff. She reached for the third one and pulled it out. It was five inches deep and lined with black velvet material. Neatly displayed inside were all sorts of vibrators and various sized dildos and butt plugs. She had metal and fuzzy handcuffs, rubber and metal cock rings, and a slew of G-spot stimulators. She even had a strap-on harness. The other drawers were filled with whips, feathers, chains, blindfolds, mouth gags, numerous latex outfits, and assorted bottles and tubes of lubricant.

Marian felt extra naughty that day and plucked out her favorite butt plug, the one made of clear safety glass with a colorful jeweled bottom. She decided against lube, preferring to feel the plug grip her. It was a wonderful way to prepare for Paul.

Reaching around, she slowly inserted the toy until it popped in and only the sparkly base was exposed. She then pranced around the room, accentuating the shift of her hips from side to side. With each step, the plug moved, giving her the most wonderful of sensations. She often dared herself to spend the day at work with the toy inside of her, but hadn't yet built up the nerve.

The dancing beauty made her way back down to the kitchen where she uncorked a bottle of cabernet sauvignon and flipped through Saturday's mail. With time to kill, the wait made her want it more. She grabbed the bottle and a glass and headed back upstairs. *A good soak to relax couldn't hurt.*

Marian relished every bit of the warm sudsy water while she puffed lazily on a joint, something else Paul had introduced her to. It didn't take long for her to start dreaming up scenarios for the evening. She liked Paul and was grateful that he had helped her open up sexually. He would always hold a special place in her vagina.

With her eyes closed and her mind flying high, she thought about Paul and how he knew her body so intimately. He knew exactly where and how to touch her and, more importantly, how to give her the most wonderful feelings. She absolutely adored the way he made her quiver when he kissed her lips lightly. She loved it even more when his tongue dotted her neck. But the best was when he would let his fingers linger along the outside of her folds before letting them slip between them to her happy button.

Her coral nipples responded quickly to the pinching and pulling. Soon she had both hands fondling, thoroughly enjoying the foreplay before the foreplay.

Even though she had completely submerged herself in the tub, she could still feel her wetness increasing. With her eyes closed and her body limp, she encouraged her fingers to explore every part of her landscape. *God, that feels great.*

Yes, everything felt great right then. Marian was in heaven, enjoying every bit of it—until the obvious presented itself. If both of her hands were busy with her nipples, then whose hand was busy between her legs?

3

She tried to scream. She gave it her all. But the orange gag strapped to her mouth had done a wonderful job of shutting Marian up. She lay flat on her back, tied to her bed with the same leather straps she had enjoyed many times before. She twisted and turned from side to side but could not free herself. Her head hurt and her eyes were crusty. The last thing she remembered, before awakening, was a cloth being pressed onto her face.

"That's the downside of being into kink," the stranger said, startling her. "You never know if the other person will forget the *safe* word."

The blond man sat casually on the chaise lounge in the corner of the bedroom. She was surprised to see him and thought for second she had smoked too much whacky weed, but the bindings holding her legs open were a firm indication that she was wrong.

Her legs were tied in a way that she could not close them. She felt exposed as he stared between them. He noticed the toy still inside her and waved a finger. "You're a naughty one, aren't you?"

He stood up, fixed his brown corduroy blazer, and straightened his khaki pants before walking around the bed toward her walk-in closet. "You have such fun toys. Many I've never seen before." He disappeared for a moment and then reappeared holding something in his hand. "This one is my favorite. It's genius."

Marian's eyes widened when she saw what he had returned with.

He walked toward her and sat near the edge of the bed. His eyes soaked up her nakedness, paying extra attention to the details between her legs. He breathed in, chest expanding. "I can smell your scent." He breathed deeply again. "Fear. It excites you."

Tears flowed as she shook her head from side to side. The straps dug deeper into her wrists and ankles. He held the gift Paul had bought her last month—the only one she refused to use. The one she even considered throwing away.

He moved closer as she desperately tried to scoot away, her legs flailing hopelessly. Marian let out more muffled cries for help. Her eyes, wide and wet, begged for him not to.

"You haven't tried this, have you?" he said.

Marian shook her head, hoping he would understand.

He did. The stranger reached up between her legs.

Marian screamed at the unthinkable. Her body, now rigid, shook uncontrollably. Her face drained itself to an ashen white. Her fists tightened into balls and her nails cut into her palms. As much as she tried, as much as she wanted to, she could not tear her eyes away from his hand, from what he held.

And in an instant, before she could gasp, she watched his hand thrust forward.

4

"It's a fist."

Detective Vince Solis had bent down near the bed and looked straight up between Marian Ward's legs. The lifelike piece of rubber was still lodged inside her vagina.

"A what?"

Solis motioned with his hand. "You know. A rubber fist."

Detective Ray Madero stepped forward for a closer look and saw an object sticking out of her. "How can you tell?"

"Played with one in a porn shop once," he said while standing up and fixing his jacket. "It's like a dildo only in the shape of a real arm, and the part inside of her, it's shaped into a balled fist. Except I think this one is a double fist."

Madero crinkled his eyebrows. "Why buy a fake one? What's wrong with the one she's already got at the end of her arm?"

"Why buy a fake cock or a pussy? People get off on it." Solis knelt again next to the body.

Madero shook his head. "I'll tell you why; women don't have cocks, so it makes sense to buy one. But she," he pointed at her, "she's already got a hand."

Solis looked back up at his partner. "Did it ever occur to you that maybe she can't reach with her own fist?"

Madero's fat head pondered the conundrum for a few seconds before he waived off Solis. "If she can wipe her own ass, she can reach."

• • •

"Reach what?" I asked as Wilkinson and I entered the bedroom. The two detectives turned toward us. They both had ignorance scrawled across their face. The one standing showed his intelligence first. "Miss, this is a crime scene."

They always do that, assume I couldn't possible be there for the crime. I didn't get it. We were dressed in suits, though I thought I looked cuter in mine than Wilkinson did in his. We made it past all the uniforms downstairs but still the idiot couldn't connect the dots that I might be somebody.

Unbelievable. I whipped my badge out. "FBI. I'm Agent Abby Kane. This is my partner, Agent Trey Wilkinson."

The detective who had spoken sauntered toward me with a stupid smirk on his face. He looked roughly six feet tall and probably had about three hundred pounds on me. I may have been short, but I had a powerful uppercut that was perfectly aligned with what had to be his tiny set of balls. *Before my father left Ireland, he was the best bare-knuckle brawler to ever come out of his town. Did I mention that?*

"Look. This is our case," he said. "We appreciate your help, but it's not needed."

That's when he tried to be funny and patted me on the head. I grabbed his hand and yanked down, forcing it back at the wrist. I had him immobilized and crying like a baby in just a few seconds. With him bent over and his face closer to my height, I leaned in. "I'm not a dog. Don't ever pet me."

"You fucking psycho bitch. Let go of me," he yelped.

Wilkinson stepped in just as I winked at the crybaby and forced him off to the side. "Let's all calm down here."

"Tell that bitch—"

Wilkinson grabbed the detective by his suit and pushed him back into the wall. "Watch your mouth."

"All right. Everybody calm down," the other detective spoke up. "Relax, pal." He stepped between Wilkinson and the other man and separated them. He then faced me with tired eyes. "I'm Detective Vince Solis," he said with his hand extended. He seemed like the smarter of the two. He was evenly tanned and wore a mustache. "That's my partner, Detective Ray Madero. Look, we got off on the wrong foot. Let's start over."

I shook Solis' hand and then walked over to the body. "What do you guys know so far?"

Solis joined me near the bed. "This woman had an appetite for kink. She's got drawers filled with this stuff."

"Besides her sexual tastes, got anything else?"

"As you can see from the sheets, she bled out. If you look closely, you'll see there are three tiny incisions." Solis pointed with a pen to her neck and then her legs. "One along the carotid artery in the neck and one on the femoral artery in each leg. She drained quickly."

I bent down for a closer look. "And this rubber object?"

"It's a fist. Doesn't look like it played a role in her death. Below that is a butt plug. Killer might have been screwing around with her beforehand," Solis said.

"Any idea who she is?" I asked as I stood up and faced him.

"She's some big shot over at Chrysler, Marian Ward. Every once in a while she's on TV or in the paper."

I turned to the only uniform in the room. "Were you the first on the scene?"

"Yes, ma'am."

"Call me Agent Kane," I said with a smile.

"Sorry. The pasty guy on the couch downstairs found her and called it in."

"Anybody talk to him yet?"

"I talked to him a little just to get a sense of what happened." The young officer took out his notebook. "His name is Paul Poole. He's an engineer at Ford. Said they met at some automotive function. They had been seeing each other for about six months, though he says it was mostly booty calls. Oh, he admits to turning her on to the BDSM life. Anyway, he said she called him on his cell and invited him over tonight."

"He took his time?" I asked.

"No. He was on his way back from Kalamazoo and had about three hours of drive time left." He scanned his notes again. "Uh, he said when he got here, he followed her trail of clothes upstairs and found her like that."

"He had a key to the house?"

The uniform shook his head. "He said the door was unlocked. He figured she had left it open for him."

"Do us a favor; make sure Mr. BDSM doesn't leave and no one talks to him before I do."

The uniform nodded again and then hurried downstairs.

I turned to Solis. "What are you thinking?"

"No sign of breaking and entering. Whoever did this knew her or had access to the house."

"Maybe she's such a horn dog she decided to fit another guy in before her main squeeze got here," Madero added.

Tiny ball man not helping.

"Forensics just arrived. We'll know more once they're able to give this place a sweep. They might find another print or something we overlooked," Solis added. He then took a step closer to me. "Agent Kane, I gotta ask. Why is the FBI involved and *how* did you guys find out about this crime scene so fast?"

5

"I was hoping you could tell us," I said. No point in holding back our agenda. "Our supervisor ordered us to fly to Detroit today. We knew coming out here had something to do with a potential serial killer. Our briefing isn't until tomorrow morning, but when we landed we got instructions to head over to this address right away."

Solis looked at Madero for a second and then back at me. "That's all you know?"

Wilkinson and I nodded. Solis motioned for everyone to follow him out of the room. We huddled at the end of the hallway, away from the CSI crew that had just appeared.

"This is what we know," Solis said. "Two months ago, a body pops up. Old homeless guy in an alley near Corktown—"

"Corktown?" I said

"Yeah, it's a small neighborhood west of downtown Detroit. Anyway, this guy has the same M.O. as our vic here, minus the fist. A month later, another body pops up. Middle-aged guy, fishing on the shores of Lake St. Clair. Again, same M.O. minus the fist."

"Wait. You're Birmingham police. Aren't these other cases out of your jurisdiction?"

Solis nodded. "They are."

I shook my head. "I don't understand. Why are you keeping tabs on them?"

"We're not," Madero added.

"Here's a little background for you." Solis pointed at Madero and then himself. "We're both new to the precinct. I'm from Jersey. Madero here is from Tampa. We've both been in the city maybe a year, so we have no history; no one knows us. But get this: we're sharing old war stories with the desk sergeant when he starts to tell us about the original Corktown murders, took place maybe fifteen years ago. A couple was found dead—cut and bled out."

"Like our vic here," I said.

"Yeah," he said. "But nobody was ever brought in. Seemed like the case was headed for the filing cabinet marked 'unsolved'. Anyway, all was quiet for six months, and then bam—a few more bodies, same M.O."

"In Corktown?" Wilkinson asks.

Solis nods. "Soon after, more bodies pop up. A couple in Detroit this time, same M.O. Next thing you know, Detroit's got a massive serial killer problem. This guy is terrorizing the place, leaving bodies left and right. Male, female—all ages. All told, maybe forty to fifty victims over a five-to-six-year period. All of them killed the same way, with an incision to the neck or legs and then left to bleed out. Of course, minus—"

"The fist. Yeah, I get it. So what happened to this killer?"

"They finally caught the guy trying to pull off a bank heist with his girlfriend. He killed fourteen people during the botched robbery."

"So they caught the guy. Case solved, right?" I asked.

Solis shrugged. "Appears that way, except…"

"Bodies are starting to turn up with the same M.O.," I said as I shifted my weight to one leg.

Solis nodded.

"It's the higher-ups who connected the dots?" Wilkinson asked.

"That's what we're thinking. Had Madero and I not chatted with the desk sergeant, this M.O. wouldn't have stood out to us. This is probably why you guys were called in."

I turned to Wilkinson. "Why us? The Bureau has local agents here."

"You know, I remember hearing about this case," he said. "The press nicknamed the guy 'The Doctor.' Anyway, I believe the local field office lent its support, and like Solis said, they ended up catching the guy. But why we're investigating instead of them seems strange."

"And they called us before this murder, the third, ever happened," I added. "Seems like there's more to this than what's being said. Two murders shouldn't spook them."

Solis put his palms up in front of him. "Hey, don't look at us. It's clear we're being kept out of the loop."

I chewed on my bottom lip. "Any other connection between her, the guy fishing on a lake, or the homeless person?"

"Nothing," he said. "Take away the incisions and these are three separate cases. Also the 'serial' word is forbidden for now. As far as the citizens of Detroit and the press are concerned, it's a whacky copycat that we're closing in on. Nothing to worry about."

"Maybe the killer is checking off a bucket list—you know, a person from different categories." Madero added.

Again, not helping.

I shook my head. "The killer seems educated. He must have had some sort of medical training, enough to know how the human body operates. These incisions are meant to drain a body as fast as possible." I headed back into the room and took another long look at the victim. "There has to be a reason why he's mimicking the original killer's M.O."

"We have yet to figure that one out," Solis said as he came up behind me. "Perhaps that's where you guys come in."

I turned to the three men. "Most serial killers have a motive behind each kill they make. They hate women, or they're ridding the world of jerks."

"So what's this guy's beef?" Solis asked.

"Not sure, but I'm betting there's an agenda. There's a reason why this person choose to copy the M.O. of a known serial killer."

"Maybe he's paying homage," Wilkinson said.

6

That same night.

"I'm home."

"Daaaaddyyy!" The two young boys charged down the tiled hallway to the front door and were scooped up, one in each arm, by the tall man.

"Where were you?" the oldest boy asked.

"Daddy had business to take care of. Boring stuff, you wouldn't want to know. But I'm home now," said Preston Carter, looking at his watch. "It's beyond your bedtimes."

A woman wearing wire-framed glasses walked into the foyer. She had chestnut-brown hair that fell just below her shoulders, and her eyes were a shade darker than a blue lagoon. She had on form-fitting jeans and a sheer blouse, and her body showed no sign that she had borne any children at all.

"It is, but they wanted to stay up until you came home." Katherine Carter gave her husband a kiss as he lowered the boys to the floor.

"Eeewwww," they groaned.

"Now, Jackson, Lorenzo. What did we agree to do as soon as Daddy got home?"

"Brush our teeth and get ready for bed," they said in unison.

The little one begged. "Mommy, can't we stay up just a little longer with Daddy?"

She looked at her husband. It would be his call.

"Here's what we'll do; you two go brush your teeth and I'll come by and read you a bedtime story. Sound good?"

Both boys cheered and raced each other up the stairs. After they disappeared, Katherine turned to her husband. "We had spaghetti for dinner. Should I fix you a plate?"

He patted his stomach and shook his head. "Sounds tempting but I stopped for a bite on the way home. I'm afraid I might explode."

"Well, you can have it for lunch tomorrow."

Preston pointed up the stairs. "I'm going to freshen up and get the boys into bed. I'll be back down."

Katherine smiled before turning and heading back into the kitchen. The two met when Katherine was a freshman at Oakland University. It wasn't long before afternoon coffee turned into weeknight dinners, which led to weekend getaways. They dated for five years, until she got pregnant. That's when they decided to marry.

Preston double-stepped it up the stairs, a sign that he was still fit at forty-five, even after a couple of chili dogs. He stopped by the hall bathroom where his sons were busy brushing their teeth. "Hurry up and pick out a book. We'll rally in Jackson's room in a few minutes."

He continued down the hall to the master bedroom and closed the door behind him. He hung up his jacket, slipped off his pants, and replaced them with a fresh T-shirt and sweatpants. In the master bath, Preston washed his hands and splashed water on his face. He ran his hand through his thick blond hair, checking the length, looking for the occasional white strand.

He stopped just short of leaving the room and headed over to the bed, where he retrieved a small metal box from under his side. He fiddled with the combination lock for a bit before it opened. Inside were two boxes of disposable scalpels and a box containing latex gloves. He plucked out two gloves and picked a scalpel. He then opened the closet and tucked them into the inside pocket of his blazer. *Always be prepared.*

He exited the bedroom. "What are we reading, boys?"

7

It was well after midnight when we left the crime scene. Making the trek from the burbs to downtown that night wasn't an option we were keen on. Instead, we found a hotel in the area and got two rooms for the night.

The next morning, we exited the lobby a little before eight. The temperature outside had already soared to eighty-five degrees. I imagined it would only get hotter in the city and the humidity would start its frizz assault on my hair.

According to the hotel concierge, Central Precinct was a straight shot from Birmingham—about a forty-minute drive along Woodward Avenue. Wilkinson drove our rental, as usual.

"You know, we could have left later, if you weren't ready."

"What are you talking about?" I asked as I applied my makeup. "I was ready."

"Doesn't look like it."

"Oh, Wilky, stop being a grouch. I know you like to watch me put on my lipstick," I said, smiling while I flipped the visor back up.

"Also, you should learn to drive one of these days," he said, shooting me a look.

"But you're so good at it."

"Don't butter me up. You need to learn."

"You know, when I was a detective in Hong Kong—"

"Another Hong Kong story. This should be good."

I stopped and shot him a raised eyebrow. "Are you going let me finish or are you going to keep rolling your eyes like a little teenage girl?"

"Fine. Talk."

"My partners always drove because, in my society, the men drove." I pointed at my chest. "I wanted to drive. They wouldn't let me."

"I'm teaching you how to drive when we get back to San Francisco. I'll insist you drive from then on to make up for all the times you were discriminated against in Hong Kong."

"Great. Can't wait." I folded my arms across my chest. "I hope you're patient. I'm a slow learner."

They say when you fight with the opposite sex it means you like them. Did we really like each other? Maybe. Also, I still wasn't sure how to tell him I had gotten my driver's license three months ago. What can I say? I liked being a passenger.

I pointed at a McDonald's. "Pull into the drive through."

"Why?"

"Because you're always like this when you haven't had your morning coffee."

"Like what?" Wilkinson scoffed.

"Exactly," I said. "Plus I could use some hot water for my green tea." I always kept a tin of loose leaf with me. Even though I had acquired my father's taste for Jameson, my mother made sure I developed an addiction to the green elixir. Maybe that explained my eye color.

"It must have been tough for you at the start," he said after a few sips.

"What do you mean?"

"You know, when you first got into law enforcement."

"It wasn't easy, but I managed."

"I'd say. Chief Inspector in charge of Organized Crime, was it?"

"Organized Crime and Triad Bureau. Why the sudden interest?"

"Well, you haven't spoken much about that."

"What do you want to know? That when I got the job, I didn't get a round of drinks after work or a celebratory lunch? That it was rumored the only orders the men wanted to hear me shout were, 'Harder,' and, 'Don't stop'?"

"No, not at all. That's terrible."

I turned to Wilkinson. "I'm sorry. Look, I know you're not like those men. It was a bittersweet time in my life."

"Was it always like that?"

"No, it actually got better when I saved my old partner from having his head blown off."

"What happened?"

"My department had targeted a small Triad gang in the Sham Shui Po district. The plan was to grab as many of the members as we could at six different locations before sunrise. My old partner and I were hitting the same residence. We punched through the door with a battering ram and caught them sleeping. It was a pretty easy roundup, until I saw a young male jump out a window with my partner not far behind."

"And you followed them both right out the window."

"Yup. Anyway, I ran down an alleyway until I reached an open doorway. Inside, I saw my partner with his arms up and a shotgun a finger's length from his face."

"He got the jump on your partner?"

"He did, don't ask me how. I took one look at the gang member's shifting eyes and knew what he was thinking; *Blow this guy away, then take out the girl.*"

"What happened?"

I chuckled a bit and shook my head.

"What's so funny?"

"I don't know what I was thinking but I jumped to the side like that movie, the one with Keanu Reeves..."

"Wait, you mean *The Matrix*?"

"Yeah, except I only had the one gun."

Wilkinson laughed and batted his palms against the steering wheel. "Don't bullshit me. Tell me you did not reenact the fricken *Matrix* to save your partner—"

"Ex-partner."

"Okay, your ex-partner's life."

"I did. And guess what? It worked."

Wilkinson shook his head; he still had a fat grin on his face. I was laughing, too. Hearing myself retell the story, it sounded incredibly stupid.

"So what happened next?" he asked.

I took a moment to catch my breath. "Well that stupid move caught the guy by surprise. He did a double take, enough time to give me the jump on him. I was able to squeeze off two rounds before crashing down on my shoulder. The first shot took out his trigger hand. The second one slammed into his face."

"Bullshit. For real?"

"If I had missed, do you honestly think I would be in this car sitting next to you?"

Wilkinson looked at me and smiled. "Damn, you really are the shit."

We both exploded into more laughter.

Okay, so we do really get along, but we're professionals. We respect one another, and that's as far as whatever this is will go.

8

We reached the station at nine sharp. Before exiting our vehicle, we cleared ourselves of the giggles and restored our professional demeanor. We expected to meet with the commanding officer that morning but it turned out that wouldn't be the case.

Shortly after, we entered the building, a stocky gentleman in a dark suit needing tailoring greeted us. Clothing aside, he seemed pleasant and had a nice smile.

"Agent Kane. Agent Wilkinson. Welcome to Detroit. I'm Lieutenant Roy White."

We shook hands and smiled. "Thanks for inviting us out, Lieutenant White," I said.

"No, thank you for coming." He then turned around. "Follow me; everybody's waiting."

Everybody?

White kept a fast pace as his shoes click-clacked on the tiled floors. "We've heard a lot about you, Agent Kane. Hong Kong's loss is our gain."

"Thanks, but I just did my job."

The precinct was housed in a fairly old building with lots of beige. It did, however, appear to have a buzz to it. The public had started to trickle inside, filing complaints, mostly about neighbors or getting booked. Memories from my early years with the force flooded my head. I smiled, but I didn't miss it.

We followed the lieutenant through two large, wooden doors. Inside I saw a long rectangular conference table surround by suits that weren't smiling. I didn't do a head count, but it looked like twelve grumpy men sitting around a table. We were directed toward two open chairs in the middle.

A clearing of a throat captured everyone's attention. I looked at the man who sat at the head of the table. His face was a look of fierceness, hardened from years of wearing the uniform, I supposed. He introduced himself as Chief of Police, Reginald Reed, Detroit Police Department. I was a bit surprised by his presence in the room actually, and slightly impressed. But the surprises didn't stop there.

The introductions continued around the table. The chiefs of police for Birmingham, Royal Oak, Grosse Pointe, Madison Heights and many more were all in attendance. I didn't expect their best. Were we in the right room? As the chiefs continued, I felt a buzzing in my pocket. I pulled out my cell. Lucy had sent me a text. "Ryan call me dog face."

Ever since I taught her how to text on Po Po's phone, it had been nonstop. I sent Ryan a text. "Stop calling your sister dog face."

I tucked my phone away just as the last chief started to introduce himself.

"You got someone else you want to text before we continue?" he asked, glaring.

I had made a new rule for myself when we moved to the States—I would always take the time to respond to my kids; call it *Operation Better Mother*. "Sorry, classified stuff. Your name?"

The chief stared me down for a moment longer before continuing. His intimidation tactics had no effect on me. I had once worked for Hong Kong Police. I glanced at Wilkinson; he looked confused, probably wondering the same thing I had—why the grumpy order of police chiefs had gathered for us. But I suspected the reason was that we were about to be thrown into a hornet's nest.

9

The chiefs looked uncomfortable in the oversized leather chairs. No good trying to hide the mood in the room. It was serious, bordering on gloom, and apparent no one wanted to be there. I started to think I didn't want to either.

"If I could have everyone's attention," Reed spoke up. The leader of this shindig was about to start the briefing. He looked at Wilkinson. "Agent Kane." And then me. "Agent Wilkinson."

Wilkinson beat me to the punch and corrected the chief. "I'm Agent Wilkinson. She's Agent Kane."

The silence and the flat look on everyone's faces told me they expected Agent Kane to be tall and broad-shouldered. What they got instead was a short, green-eyed firecracker looking up at them from across the table. I was used to it. So long as I wasn't publically denied any ride at an amusement park, my height never bothered me.

Reed cleared his throat and then shifted in his seat for the third time. "I'm sure you have questions. I can start by answering the ones I know you'll ask."

This should be good.

Reed looked to be in his fifties—still young, but the worry lines across his forehead told another story. He clasped his weathered hands together and looked around the room before settling on Wilkinson and I.

"We are facing a grave situation—one we all would like to resolve quickly and quietly. What we discuss today must not leave this room. Is that understood, Agent Kane and Agent Wilkinson?"

We both nodded. "It's my understanding that we're here to consult on a possible serial killer," I said. "I'm not sure what's so secretive about that. You've only had your third body last night, which officially qualifies it."

Reed didn't blink, didn't move… but only stared until he spoke again. "About seven years ago, we had a serial killer terrorize the city of Detroit and many of the surrounding towns. This went on for five… long… years." Both hands helped him emphasize his point. "Forty-five victims, most of them in Detroit. Do you know what that does to a city, to the people?"

I wasn't sure I wanted to speak up. The seriousness with which Reed had delivered the information only filled my head with more questions seeking answers. "Our understanding is you caught him."

Some of the chiefs shifted in their chairs as they looked toward Reed.

"We don't want a repeat. Every chief of police you see here today represents a city that had victims the last go-round. Some of them, including me, even have the pleasure of participating in the second go-round. We're all in agreement; we don't want this to turn into another massacre. We believe we have a copycat on our hands."

"Well, if you think it's just a copycat, seems like you could throw enough manpower at it to put this to bed quickly."

"Agent Kane, we were told by your superiors we would have your full cooperation. Did I misunderstand this?"

Note to self: check with Special Agent Reilly on why we were sent. "You do have our cooperation. I'm sorry if I led you to believe something else." *Why is he so sensitive?*

"We're giving you and your partner full authority on this case. No matter what city a body pops up in, if it has the same M.O., you two will be the senior investigators on it."

Take on every case? Oh, that sounds like fun. What else can I do around here? Hand jobs for the table? "What about the other detectives?" I asked.

"They'll still work the case. Look at them as extra pairs of eyes and hands. Don't be afraid to use them. Everyone here is behind this. Any resource you need, case files, access to evidence—Lieutenant White is your go-to guy, but feel free to reach out to any of us. Agent Kane, you come highly recommended. We're looking to you to nip this in the bud."

Don't forget about the white male I walked into the room with; he's helping too. I never thought I would see a room full of chiefs so scared of their own shadows. It worried me a bit. *It's not normal. Something isn't right here.*

As usual with briefings like that one, I had been thrown into a situation where I had the full support of everyone, so long as I stuck to the support they were comfortable giving. I also had complete control, so long as I stuck within the parameters of what they felt warranted enough control. Lastly, I had access to all the information they thought I needed to solve the case, not a file more. I knew the routine. It was bull, but I had never let it get in the way in the past and I wouldn't this time.

Wilkinson and I thanked them with smiles long enough to carry us out of the room, not a step further. My partner leaned in and whispered, "What sort of clusterfuck did we just get handed?"

"The worst kind," I said. "There's more going on than the chiefs are letting on. That's another case we need to crack. I have a feeling it's the answer to catching our guy."

10

White led us down a corridor away from the public areas of the precinct. "I'm gonna set you guys up near me. It's quieter over here."

Is that so you can keep a close eye on us?

He opened the door to a small office. We peeked inside and saw two desks, two chairs, and a large board for posting or writing on.

"This was an old storage area but we cleaned it out and use it for interrogations every once in awhile."

I guess the cleaning didn't apply to the cobwebs hanging from the ceiling?

"It's your office now," he continued. "My humble abode is just around the corner, past the men's bathroom. Don't be afraid to stop by if you need anything or have questions." White took a step but stopped and turned back. "You guys have an idea on what kind of information you need?"

"Case files for all the previous murders and current ones to start with," I said. Just then my cell rang. It was Po Po. I asked Wilkinson if he could continue as I stepped outside the office and walked a few steps away.

"Po Po, is everything all right?"

"Yeah, everything is fine. I'm calling to see when you're coming home."

"Wait, there's a lot of static. Hang on." I walked toward the front of the building. *Much better.* "I think I'm going to be out here for a while. I'll see what I can do about coming back for a visit."

Po Po grunted and then said, "Lucy wants to talk."

I could hear the phone exchanging hands and then the sound of heavy breathing. "Hi, Mommy. I miss you."

"Mommy misses you too, Lucy. Are you getting ready for school?"

"Yes."

"Good. You'll have to show me what you did today when I get home."

"When are you coming back?"

"Mommy doesn't know yet."

"Oookay."

Before I could say anything else, I heard rustling and then silence. I walked back into the office. It smelled of turpentine. Wilkinson had already taken a seat at one of the desks. "The lieutenant is having all the case files delivered here. He said to give it an hour or two. Oh, and I cleaned off your chair."

"Why? What was—"

"You don't want to know."

• • •

We spent the next few days holed up in the tiny office. I started to feel like a regular at the precinct—punching the clock and getting to know the vending machines. I even kept a stash of green tea in the break room.

A couple of uniforms had delivered a mountain of stuffed banker boxes to us that first day. Every single one of them was filled with files from the previous and current case, so we were told. Without an obvious starting point, we just grabbed a file and started to read.

We dubbed all the victims before the Comerica Bank heist "pre-bank" murders. Anyone killed after that we called "post-bank." It made it easier since there seemed to be no rhyme or reason to how the files were organized. I assumed all the information we needed was there; we just had to make sense of it.

It wasn't until the third day that we found what we were looking for, something we should have had from the very start of the investigation.

"Got it," Wilkinson waved a file in the air.

We had been searching for the original killer's case file from the moment we got the boxes. Up until that point, we had developed a good grasp of who the victims were, but we didn't know much about him.

"Michael 'Blade' Garrison," Wilkinson read aloud. "Grew up in Sterling Heights. Did a year at Oakland Community College—"

"No med school?"

"Nope, not that I can tell."

"Strange, you'd think this guy would have had a medical background given the way his victims died."

"He could have gotten his information in a public library or online."

Self-taught? "What else is in the file?"

"No previous arrests until he was caught robbing the bank."

"You're kidding me, right?" *How did he get so good at being a bad guy without slipping up?* "This guy terrorizes the city for five years, and it's not until he robs a bank that they catch him. That make any sense to you?"

Wilkinson threw his hands up. "Why on earth would a serial killer suddenly want to rob a bank? It's not like the skills transfer over."

I listened as he continued to read out loud. "In a nutshell, he tried to rob the main branch of the Comerica Bank. Things went wrong. The police showed up. He took hostages and ended up killing fourteen people by either shooting them or cutting them before SWAT stormed the bank. He was found guilty of those murders, attempted robbery, and a slew of other stuff. Looks like that's how they put him away. Sounds like amateur hour if you ask me."

"What about the other murders?" I asked.

Wilkinson continued. "Well, it says he confessed to them."

I picked up a file on one of the victims. "This one says, "Closed. Case solved." I grabbed another. "Hmm, says the same thing here too." It appeared as though Garrison did indeed confess to all the murders.

"Sounds like the dream case," Wilkinson said. "Talk about caving in."

My gut didn't agree with what we had discovered. The guy they arrested for robbing the bank and killing the hostages turned out to be the serial killer they'd hunted for five years. Talk about miracles.

Wilkinson looked at his watch and stood up. "You want the same thing?"

I looked at my watch; it was noon. "I'm sorry. I like chili dogs as much as the next guy, but I can't eat another one of those things. It's making me constipated."

Wilkinson pulled his face back. I knew he hated it when I talked about bodily functions. He somehow had it in his head that there were only two things that ever came out of a woman's body: babies and pee.

11

We took a two-block walk to the Coney Island restaurant where Wilkinson had been buying the chili dogs. Turns out they sold salads, too. *Wish I knew*. There were a couple of open booths, so we parked our butts in one.

"What are you thinking so far?" Wilkinson asked.

I scrunched my lips together before answering. "It's like they took whatever they had and stitched the case closed."

"You saying the stitching's crooked?"

"That's what I'm saying."

"He did confess. Whether it was coerced, who knows? Does it matter if corners were cut on his case?"

"Good question," I said with a head tilt. "The case against Garrison may not have been airtight, but everyone around here bought into it. He's in jail."

Wilkinson nodded at me. Just then, the waitress arrived and took our order. I waited until she was out of earshot before speaking again. "Let's come at this a different way. All of the previous victims died from excessive bleeding, but not all of them were cut the same way. Some only had incisions to the carotid artery while others included the femoral artery as well."

"You thinking there's a reason for that?"

"Well, they bleed faster." I sat back in the booth and flipped through a couple of case files I had brought along. "Hmm, just as I had suspected."

"What?"

"Based on the sampling I have here, the victims that sustained three cuts were found in secluded areas, like a house or an alley. The victims that were found in public spaces had fewer cuts."

"So Garrison didn't always have time."

"The more public the venue, the faster he had to be."

"One cut, two cuts at the most."

I nodded as I took a sip of my iced tea. "He needed to know exactly where to hit them. An incision elsewhere wouldn't kill the person. Might even end up being a superficial wound."

"And that's where the medical training comes into play."

"Exactly. Garrison had to be skilled. Which means our copycat is as well. Either that or he's just some lucky nut slicing people up."

Wilkinson looked at his notes. "Well, every one of our post-bank victims had three cuts. The house and alley are secluded. They found the fisherman's body on the shore of Lake St. Clair. It might have been a secluded area. But where does this theory lead us? This guy is a bit more selective?"

I shrugged, not sure if that angle took us anywhere either. "One thing is true; whether it's one cut or two or three, he still has to know what he's doing, because the incisions are so precise."

The waitress placed a plate with two chili dogs and fries in front of Wilkinson and a fried chicken salad in front of me. His plate had more chili than bun and dog, like a big pile of slop. I watched him pick up the bun, and the chili poured off of it in glops. Yellow cheesy strands kept the chili in the plate connected to the chili on his hot dog. He opened wide, but still the thickness of that cylindrical meal was wider than his mouth and left a ring of chili around his lips. *If he wasn't so damn good looking…*

I dug in to my salad. As I chewed, another thought replayed itself in my head. I tapped my fork at the edge of my bowl. "You know what keeps striking me as motive for Garrison?"

Wilkinson eyed me as he shoved the remaining half of his chili dog into his mouth.

"He had to enjoy watching people bleed to death. There wasn't any connection between his victims except how he killed them. He had to be getting off on the blood."

"Makes sense," Wilkinson managed as he finished swallowing. "So what does that mean?" Wilkinson asked. "That our current killer likes the blood version of Old Faithful? Also, why are we spending so much time figuring out a case that's been put to bed?"

"Trust me on this one. The more we understand Garrison, the more we'll understand our copycat."

Wilkinson inhaled the last of his second chili dog and chewed. I poured more ranch dressing on my salad and mixed it in. I could sense Wilkinson wasn't buying everything I said, but as my partner, he was willing to go along for the ride. I appreciated his trust. "This person could have been studying our original guy. According to the newspaper articles, some case details that should have remained off-limits were released. It was completely possible for someone to pick up where Garrison left off."

Wilkinson swallowed the last of his fries and brushed his hands off. "Why go through the trouble of making the kills so exact? Most copycats are sloppy about it. This person is dead on."

"Maybe he wants people to think the killer was never caught in the first place."

We pondered our conversation while I finished off my salad.

Wilkinson broke the silence. "Where does it all go—the food?"

I shrugged, knowing he meant that as a compliment. My body was more athletic than curvaceous. Though, what I wouldn't do to have more booty. Just for once I'd love to wiggle it, just a little bit. I wiped my mouth and reapplied my lipstick.

"You know, Garrison is being held in a prison not too far from us," Wilkinson said.

"I guess it's time for our first field trip."

12

Grosse Pointe was an enclave for wealthy Detroit. A lot of old money resided in the neighborhood but the *nouveau riche* had started to take over. Either way, Preston Carter's SUV, a Mercedes, allowed him to blend perfectly.

He parked his vehicle near the corner of East Jefferson Avenue and St. Clair Street and sat comfortably inside, hidden from the pummeling sun thanks to a large oak tree. Etta James crooned softly from the sound system as Preston hummed along. His windows were down, allowing the lazy breeze from the lake to carry its scent by him. He had been waiting for close to an hour with an eye on Strafford Lane, across the street. It led to a quiet cul-de-sac near the lake's edge.

Almost time for another lesson, Preston chuckled. He was excited about the work he did. He felt people had to learn that there were consequences for their actions—that they had to be kept in check, made aware of such things. *It's my job to teach them.*

Ten minutes later, an old pickup truck with lawn equipment in the back squealed to a stop at the corner of E. Jefferson and Strafford. The gardener was done for the day. Preston knew he had two hours before the man of the house would return from work. He started his engine and drove to the two-story brick house with white trim at the end of Strafford. Tall hedges surrounded the property to keep the neighbors at bay, with the exception of the side of the house that faced the lake.

Preston pulled his SUV into the driveway; the gate was on the fritz and therefore wide open. Of course, he had known that. A few seconds later, he rang the doorbell and waited.

The door creaked open, enough for a woman in her early fifties to peek out. She didn't seem worried that a stranger had entered the property and stood outside her door. Preston was a good-looking man with a full head of hair. He stood six feet with proportionate weight. His attire was conservatively wealthy, and most importantly, he had a charming smile.

"May I help you?" the woman said.

"Sorry to bother you, Mrs. Walters… it *is* Mrs. Walters, correct?"

"Yes, that's right. Do I know you?"

Preston let out a friendly chuckle and teetered back on his heels. "No, unfortunately we haven't met. I know your husband, Dennis." He stuck his hand out. "I'm Preston Carter. Pleased to meet you."

Mrs. Walters smiled, her guard completely down, as she opened the door all the way. Preston breathed in deeply. *Lilac. How refreshing.*

She wore a knee-length cream linen dress, and a single strand of pearls draped her thin neck. Her blonde locks were pulled back neatly into a bun and held in place by a jeweled pin. She seemed extremely composed, though he did detect a hint of highbrow in her demeanor.

"Well, I'm pleased to meet you, too, Preston. Call me Irene," she said as she extended her hand. A few seconds later, she wished she hadn't.

13

The Macomb Correctional Facility was a thirty-minute drive northeast of Detroit. We didn't bother to check in with Lieutenant White, preferring to take our own chances with visitation. Just as I thought, a flash of our badges got us an appointment to see Michael Garrison. *It's good to be FBI.*

After we checked our sidearms in with the officer behind the counter, we were told to have a seat. Ten minutes of kicking at the floor and reading *Time* magazines passed before a pudgy guy in a uniform approached us.

"I'm Gary Walczak, the senior corrections officer on duty. I understand you two are FBI agents and want to see inmate #04291144, Michael Garrison."

"That's correct," I said. "Will that be a problem?"

"Nah, but I need to inform you that, because of the nature of his crimes, he's kept separate from general pop. Too many guys want a crack at him for what he did. He's not even allowed in the visitor's room. We have a place where you can meet with him privately."

"That'll be fine," I said.

"Just a warning, if you hadn't already been told, he's got a quick mouth. He likes to instigate and get under your skin. It's all a game with him."

"I'll keep that in mind."

A few minutes later we were led into a twelve-by-ten room containing a metal table and two stools, all bolted to the floor. Before we could settle in, Michael Garrison shuffled into the room, handcuffed and chained at the ankles.

To be honest, he wasn't what I expected. For one, I thought he would be taller and not so skinny-jean thin. His hair was a greasy mess and he had a spotty beard. The officer sat him down and chained his handcuffs to the table.

"You guys okay?" Walczak asked.

We both nodded and then waited until the door clanked shut before addressing Garrison—only he opened his mouth first. "Who the fuck are you?"

"I'm Agent Abby Kane and this is my partner Agent Trey Wilkinson. We're with the FBI. We'd like to ask you a few questions, Michael."

"Call me Blade," he said, his eyes never leaving mine.

"All right, Blade. I want—"

"You guys fucking each other?"

The officer wasn't kidding. I took a moment to figure out a plan for that jack-hole. I knew his type—met plenty over the years. Fighting them never works. I straightened up. "Would you answer my questions if I said we were?"

"Maybe."

A smirk developed on his face. Still, his eyes never wavered. *Give and take, Abby.* I leaned forward a bit. "We're fuck buddies. Now tell me, Blade—"

"How often?" He shot back as his eyes focused on my breasts.

"At the bank, why did you kill all those people?"

Garrison looked me in the eyes once again. "I didn't kill all those people. I know everyone thinks I did but I only killed some of them."

"Fourteen people were found either shot or cut."

"Right. I shot people with a gun. I didn't cut anyone. Someone else did that shit." Garrison rubbed his runny nose and then sniffed.

"What about the other victims around town? The ones killed by The Doctor?"

His smile widened. I should have known an answer to my question wasn't coming next. "I hear Asians don't shave down below. You got a bush?"

"I do. Now, why did you move away from cutting your victims to shooting them?"

"I told you already. Fuck! I didn't cut anyone that day at the bank and I didn't cut any of those other people before that either." Garrison relaxed his posture a bit before asking, "Is it big?"

"Is what big?"

"Your bush," he said like an embarrassed teen.

"It's bushy. Do you like that?"

He nodded.

"Keep talking Blade; I might keep answering."

Garrison closed his eyes as he smacked his lips. He appeared to have gone off into fantasyland. I wanted to slap that stupid grin off his face and then shove it down his throat. I mouthed over to Wilkinson, "He's thinking of you."

From that point on, Garrison walked me through what happened that day at the bank without any interruptions. He and his girl had plans to rob the place but it went wrong. He admitted to shooting some of the hostages but someone else in the building sliced the others. He couldn't figure out who did it. Eventually that person killed his girl. That's when he lost it and started shooting all the hostages as payback, thinking if he killed them all, he would get his revenge.

At first, I thought Garrison was lying, but I believed what he said about his girlfriend. I didn't think he killed her. Maybe there was someone else. Perhaps our copycat?

"So you have no idea who else was killing the hostages?"

"I narrowed it down to this one business dude."

"What happened to him?"

"Will you let me eat you out if I tell you?"

My partner couldn't take Garrison's off-the-cuff comments any longer. "Watch it, asshole."

Garrison turned to him. "What? You think you're the only one who likes Chinese?"

Wilkinson shot from his seat and grabbed Garrison, slamming his head down onto the table. "This is your last warning."

I quickly pulled Wilkinson off. Garrison's remarks were uncalled for but nothing I couldn't ignore. I did appreciate Wilkinson's concern, though.

"What the fuck, dick?" Garrison shouted. "Remember, *you* guys wanted to talk to *me*."

I struck the table with my palm a few times. "Blade, focus! I'm asking the questions. What happened to the businessman?"

Garrison slowly turned his head to me, his eyes the last to follow. "I fucking shot him. He was the last one I took out before I was taken down."

"What about the two hostages that survived? Why not suspect them?"

"I don't know. Didn't seem the type. The business guy was cocky. But if I had the time, I would have shot those last two as well. My girlfriend was dead and everyone else needed to pay."

The metal door creaked and caught our attention. It swung open and the same corrections officer appeared, signaling the end to our time. Garrison realized the same thing and started with a barrage of sexual questions, hoping I would indulge him and provide more fodder for his playtime than I already regrettably had.

"Come on. Show me it. Really quick."

The corrections officer piped up. "Shut up, Garrison, or else I'm throwing you in the hole."

Right before they exited, Garrison opened his mouth once more. I honestly don't know what he said. All I know is I heard the "C" word and it set me off. I exploded across the room and pinned him up against the wall. I stood on my toes to get closer to his ear and whispered. "You know, if you had said please instead of calling me that name, I would have gladly shown it to you."

The look on Garrison's face was priceless. I could hear him yelling, "Please!" over and over as he was led away.

14

Dennis Walters had developed a routine that he rarely deviated from. Every day he left his office at 5:00 p.m. His administrative assistant had learned not to schedule anything that would keep him later. As a young executive, he had worked tirelessly, but he was nearing retirement and didn't feel like he needed to be the first one in and the last one out. He had paid his dues.

Dennis had been a car guy his entire life. Since the age of twenty-two, he had worked his way up the ranks at GM until he was the CFO. Not bad for a farm kid from Kentucky.

He thought he had the best job because he actually loved cars. He already knew he would spend his retirement rebuilding the classics. Fixing up a red 1960 Chevy Impala hooked him a few years back. He cherished that car and reserved it for Sunday drives with the wife.

As Dennis Walters neared his driveway, he saw that the gate was open. *Remember to call the maintenance guy.* He parked behind a silver SUV and thought Irene must have company, most likely one of the ladies from the Junior League. She had gotten involved with them ten years ago and had loved helping out ever since.

He heard music playing the moment he walked through the front door. It sounded familiar but he couldn't recall the name of the singer. Nonetheless, it put him in an extra happy mood. He headed to where they kept the stereo system. "Irene, I'm home." But the sitting room was empty. Dennis tilted his head as he gave the room a once over. *Weird.* It was unlike his wife to leave music playing.

"Irene?" He tried once more—still no answer. He put his briefcase down near an end table, where he noticed a CD cover—Etta James. *That's the one.* He listened for a bit longer. He tapped a foot and let his head bob a bit before heading towards the kitchen. That's where he bumped into Preston Carter, pouring himself a glass of orange juice.

"Oh, hello. I didn't think anyone was in here," Dennis said. He was a bit taken aback. His jaw hung half open as he looked around. "Are you a friend of Irene's?"

"I am. You must be Dennis," Preston said as he extended his hand across the granite-topped island between them. "I'm Preston Carter."

Dennis' face relaxed a bit as he took a few steps forward and shook the smiling stranger's hand. "Any idea where my wife might be?"

"She stepped out to the garage for a second," Preston said pleasantly. He chuckled. "It must look strange coming home to find someone you don't know helping himself to your orange juice."

Dennis clasped his hands together and flashed a smile. "Can't say that I've had this experience before. Are you with the Junior League?"

"I've heard a lot about them," Preston said as he reached up to the copper pot rack above them and removed a large cast iron skillet. "But no, I'm not with them. I'm with another organization that your wife had the pleasure of getting involved with not too long ago. It's called the I'm-Here-to-Fucking-Kill-You League."

15

When Preston arrived home later that evening, his ears sensed something was amiss. It was quiet. A house with two young boys is never quiet.

He entered by the door in the garage that led him through the laundry room. He stopped just before entering the hallway and listened. He didn't hear a gunfight between the Cowboys and the Indians or Harry Potter whizzing around on a broom. In fact, there was not a single sound that suggested the kids were home. *Strange.* He removed his shoes and moved silently through the carpeted hallway.

Preston peeked into the kitchen and saw his wife unloading the dishwasher. He walked on his tippy toes, careful not to give away his presence until he stood right behind her. He reached around her waist with both arms and pulled her against him, planting playful kisses along her neck.

Katherine squealed in delight as she fought to escape his grasp while his thumbs continued tickling both sides of her rib cage. She eventually turned herself around.

"Preston, stop. I can't take it!" she shouted, almost out of breath.

He let up and pulled her in for a long kiss before looking at his wife's eyes and quickly ribbing her once more. It took Katherine a few breaths to calm down.

"Where are the boys?" he asked.

"The Pipers'. Marcus invited them to a sleepover."

Preston raised an eyebrow and cocked his head slightly. "That means we have the house to ourselves tonight."

Katherine giggled more. "Yes. Did you have something in mind?"

Preston lifted his wife up by her behind as she wrapped her legs around his waist. She could already feel him growing. He turned around and walked out of the kitchen. One by one he climbed the stairs while he tongued her neck.

"Mmm, don't stop." Katherine enjoyed his tenderness for a bit more before asking how it went.

"You naughty girl, you. Want to know what Daddy did, do you?"

Preston kicked the master bedroom door open and laid his wife down on the bed. In between kisses, he told her all about Irene and how nice she was, until she realized how nice he wasn't. "You should've seen the fear in her eyes," Preston whispered devilishly into his wife's ear.

"Don't stop," she said.

Preston undid his belt buckle and unzipped his pants as Katherine reached inside and grabbed him. "You're so thick."

He pushed her dress up over her hips and his fingers found their wet mark. "You're so inviting. I don't know who likes this kinky talk more."

"What else?" she asked, taking a deep breath as he entered her.

"I hit her once, knocking her to the ground. Blood ran from her nose. Then I picked her up and hit her over and over," he said, accenting his words with his thrusts.

"She's a tough one," Katherine managed between breaths.

"Not really. I knocked her out after the second hit. I just enjoyed hitting her."

"You devil. How about fucking me harder?"

He was happy to oblige. "You'll love what I did next. I took her into the garage and sat her in this beautifully-restored, American, classic car. Buckled her in the front seat as if she were waiting for a driver."

"Oh, God, don't stop," Katherine moaned.

Preston increased his speed. "And then I cut her. You like that?"

"Yes!"

He grabbed Katherine's hair and pulled. "Take it. Take it all, you slut."

"Yes, I love it. Don't stop."

"The seats were white leather. I wish you could have seen it. When Dennis got home, I was in the kitchen pouring myself a cup of orange juice. Imagine that."

"Was he surprised to see you?"

"Can you feel my balls slapping against you?"

"Oh, yes. I want it bad. Stick it in my ass," she ordered.

Preston stopped and flipped his wife over onto her stomach. He spread her cheeks and licked her ready. Then he slid inside.

"Yes! Finish me off," she cried.

Preston picked up the pace again. "We made small talk. I told him Irene and I were friends. 'The Junior League,' the dumb mule suggested. He found me so charming. I reached for a skillet that hung from the rack above us, a shiny one that was hardly used. That stupid fucker didn't suspect a thing."

"My God… you're going to make me cum."

He grabbed her thick mane and pulled tightly. She was close. So was he. He kept up the pace, pushing her toward the edge. Just as she reached her point of no return, he whispered in her ear.

"You could hear his face crack when I hit him."

16

Early the next morning, Wilkinson and I headed over to the bureau's field office on Michigan Avenue. We were eager to talk to the agents who worked the Garrison case and get their take on it. I was in a good mood and looking forward to mixing it up with other agents outside of my own office—some quality G-man bonding. Every now and then, I kind of wished I had a penis.

When we got there, my happy outlook changed. A stern-looking man greeted us in reception. He had parted his hair on the side and coated it with some sort of slick product. I couldn't stop staring. *Hair helmet.*

"I'm Special Agent Tully," he said as he shook both our hands.

"I'm Agent Abby Kane and this is Agent…"

Tully spun around on his heels before I finished. "Walk with me," he ordered.

I looked at Wilkinson with my lips pursed and eyes wide open. He gave me half a shrug. We stood up and dragged our feet, purposely.

"You guys are about a month late. Agent Max and Agent Ton got relocated. One is in San Diego and the other,

Atlanta. Off the top of my head, I can't remember who went where."

"You got a number or an address for them?" I asked.

"No."

No pause, no sorry—just a quick no. *Where's the charm?* "What can you tell us about them?"

"Good guys. Quiet. Worked hard. It shocked me when I heard they wanted to leave. I thought they were happy here."

He led us to a Dutch door with a built-in counter. The plastic sign hanging above the opening of the door read, Records Division. "I figured you guys would want to pore through their files on the case."

"Thanks. We appreciate it," Wilkinson said.

Agent Tully hit the little bell on door counter a couple of times. "Hey, Joey Records."

An elderly black man appeared in the window a few seconds later. He had a big white mustache covering both lips and his cheeks bulged like a chipmunk's when he smiled.

"I need you to pull all of the Garrison case files."

The old man responded with a raspy, "Sure will," before shuffling away.

"Any idea why they were transferred?"

"Change of pace. At least that's the story they both gave. They put in for the transfer. Now if you can handle yourselves from here, I have a meeting." Tully did an about-face without waiting for an answer and disappeared around the corner.

I let out a breath. "We always get the nice ones."

Ten minutes later, Joey Records returned with four boxes on a cart. *That's it? How in-depth was their investigation?*

"Here you go," he said with a smile and a twinkle in his eye. "Just put everything back in the box and return it to me when you're finished."

I smiled at him. "Thank you."

We secured an empty office around the corner and closed the door behind us. Our initial assessment was that everything seemed to agree with what we had covered back at Central—except it was the CliffsNotes version. Nothing looked out of place, but it literally looked as though the agents stopped working the case the minute they found out Garrison was caught.

"So our guys helped out until Garrison was caught and then called it quits?"

Wilkinson glanced up from a file. "Looks that way." He must have noticed the confusion on my face. "What?"

I tucked my chin in. "Sounds a little suspect, don't you think? Why not see it through? It's not like they were taking a test and someone said, 'Pencils down. Turn in your report.' " I leaned back in my chair, willing to let the situation stew.

Wilkinson rubbed his hands together. "Dunno. Maybe it wasn't their decision."

I popped up out of my chair. "I'll be right back."

I exited the office and walked back to Records. "Hey, Joey Records."

"Yes ma'am?" Joey lowered a newspaper enough for his eyes to peek above.

"Are you sure those are all the files?"

"I am."

"Anybody else request these files?"

He frowned a bit as he slowly shook his head. "No, you two are the first since I cataloged them. Why?" he asked, folding his paper and putting it down.

"They feel a bit light. Plus, none of the cases are closed. It's like the agents stopped working on everything at once and packed it in."

Joey Records shrugged. "Sorry, sweetie. It's all I got."

He reminded me of a co-worker back in Hong Kong, Shen Wo. He was the oldest inspector on the force, always on the verge of retiring—just happy to be around. He often treated me as his granddaughter. Sweet old man.

I returned the files when we were done and then we set off looking for Tully. We found him a few minutes later in the cafeteria spending time with a coffee and a Danish. *Was this the meeting you mentioned earlier?*

"Agents. Finding everything you need?"

"I wouldn't say that. How familiar are you with the Garrison case?"

"About as familiar as I need to be. Why?" He put down the last bite of his Danish and brushed the crumbs from his fingers.

"Well, it looks as if your agents stopped working the case a day after Detroit Metro Police arrested Garrison. No follow-ups. No nothing. It's like they set the files aside and never gave it another thought."

"Doesn't surprise me. If I recall correctly, we were short staffed around that time. Any resources we could pull away from Detroit Metro Police would have helped. They had their guy."

"Is that normal procedure around here?"

"Look, Agent," he said, standing up, "I know you're this ex-hotshot detective, but this isn't Hong Kong."

"Exactly. So why are you bringing it up?" *What's wrong with these people? Aren't we all on the same team?* I didn't know what I'd said to merit that attitude, but Helmet Head was getting on my nerves.

"With all due respect, Special Agent Tully, we were asked to help with this case. We are not volunteers. Let's get that straight. Secondly—"

"Agent," Tully raised his voice, "I outrank you. Get that straight. You were given the information needed. Now, go solve the case. Good day."

Tully stood up and walked away, leaving me speechless. I could feel every eye in the room glaring. All I could do was look down. Finally, I turned to my partner. "Tell me I wasn't out of line."

Wilkinson gave me a pat on the back. "You weren't. Don't sweat it." He stood and made eye contact with everyone. A beat later, the audience went back to their business as if nothing had happened.

On our way out of the building, my cell rang. It was White. Two more bodies had popped up.

17

Detroit was exactly like one would imagine it: deserted.

During our drive to the scene, we passed a slew of empty apartment buildings and abandoned storefronts; some of the buildings I saw were burnt out. Others were partially demolished. *City porn for photographers*, I thought. Only when it's framed and in black and white do we finally see beauty and history in these once magnificent buildings. So sad.

I continued to daydream out my window as we sped past the urban blight until I experienced a sudden scene change. My view went from liquor stores to mansions in the blink of an eye. "Wait, what just happened?" I asked, turning to Wilkinson.

"Grosse Pointe is what just happened," Wilkinson said. "The divide between the poor and the rich is that welcome sign back there."

I couldn't believe it. One minute I'm staring at someone pushing a shopping cart down the street, and next I'm looking at immaculate lawns with the help riding a lawnmower.

"Manicured to perfection," Wilkinson motioned with his finger.

The address we had took us to Strafford Lane, which dead-ended at Lake St. Clair. Packed into the tiny cul-de-sac were a slew of cruisers and a CSI lab vehicle. We arrived right behind the Wayne County Medical Examiner, which was a sign the bodies hadn't been moved yet. Wilkinson parked behind the examiner's van, and I watched a portly white guy with a mustache exit the vehicle.

The area around the house had already been cordoned off, but a couple of uniforms still worked the perimeter to keep the nosy neighbors at bay. *I bet every single one of them called their home security service for extra drive-bys.*

I flashed my badge at the nearest uniform.

"Are the detectives inside the house?"

He shook his head. "The bodies aren't in the house; they're in the garage. It's a big mess in there. Blood everywhere. Might want to hike your pants up."

I thanked him for the heads-up. *What are we in for this time?* We passed a couple of uniforms on the way. One looked green in the face. *Was it that bad?*

Large fluorescent lighting brought the three-car garage to life. A group of men were huddled near an old red car, talking amongst themselves. They pivoted when they heard my heels on the driveway. Two of them I recognized right away from the Marian Ward case. *Great, Tweedle Dee and*

Tweedle Dum. I leaned over to Wilkinson. "I could have sworn those two were Birmingham police."

"It gets more interesting," he said.

The one with the mustache, not the one who tried to pet me, spoke first. "Agent Kane, Agent Wilkinson, right?"

"That's correct. Detectives Solis and Madero, right?"

"You got it."

"I thought you guys were Birmingham police," I said.

"We are, but the higher-ups ordered us to work any case associated with this killer."

"Lucky you," I said.

Solis shrugged. "I heard you two had the same luck as well."

"It appears that way." I wasn't sure if this was good or bad. On one hand it kept the number of cooks in the kitchen to a handful, but on the other hand, these two didn't seem to be all that bright.

I turned my attention to the bright red car with chrome trimmings. It was a convertible and the top was down so everyone had a clear view of the inside of the vehicle. A man in his fifties sat behind the wheel. A woman occupied the passenger seat who, I guessed, was around the same age. They were posed. He had his hands around the wheel. She was leaning in toward him. They were on a Sunday drive to nowhere. Their mouths were the eerie part; they both hung open. If you took away the waterfall of blood that ran down their necks, coloring their clothing, it could pass for an exhibit at an automobile museum.

Before I could take a step forward, Wilkinson stopped me. "Blood," he said, pointing to the floor. A large dark pool of it spread out from underneath the car. I walked over to Solis. "What do you know so far?"

"Dennis and Irene Walters are the unlucky couple. He's a bigwig at General Motors, CFO. The wife is one of those volunteer types."

"GM? Marian Ward worked for Chrysler. I wonder if they knew each other."

"Probably. It's a small town."

"Could our guy be targeting auto executives?" I asked. "You know, the whole disgruntled factory worker angle."

"Could be a grievance with the unions, or maybe these executives did something unpopular in the industry. Lots of possibilities," Wilkinson added.

I looked back at Solis. "See what you guys can dig up on these two."

"Will do," he said while walking away.

"Solis," I called out as I pointed at the two bodies, "let's finish here first."

"Right. Uh, well, both victims took trauma to the head, probably how the killer knocked them out long enough to strap them into the seats—"

"Strap?"

"Oh yeah. Come around this way." Solis motioned with his pen. "They're wearing their seat belts."

A couple of doormats had been laid across the floor to reach the vehicle. I walked over and peered inside the car. "Same incisions?"

"On the neck at least. Can't tell if they have them on the legs. We didn't want to disturb the scene before forensics arrived."

I motioned to the floor of the garage with my head. "How did so much blood end up underneath the car?"

"My guess is he cut them before placing them in the car."

"And those footprints?"

"Gardener. He found them this morning. He said when he left yesterday afternoon, the wife was still alive and the husband hadn't returned home from work yet."

I bent down and examined the blood spill closer. The edges had dried but the center still had some liquidity to it. "Timing feels about right. I'm guessing they were both killed shortly after the husband got home." I looked back up at Solis. "Anybody talk to the neighbors yet?"

"Not yet. We'll get some uniforms—"

"No uniforms. I want you and Madero talking to them. Find out what the neighbors know about these two. What time does he come home from work? Do they entertain a lot or keep to themselves? Were they liked or hated in the neighborhood? Find out if there's any gossip these people are willing to give up."

Solis nodded and walked back over to Madero. Wilkinson moved up, took his place alongside me, and peered inside the vehicle. "Garrison didn't do this. Stage people. Why would our copycat do this?"

"He could be bored," I suggested. "Serial killers kill a certain way because it feeds a need. It brings them satisfaction."

"And copycats aren't like that?"

"Not from what I've seen."

Wilkinson swallowed.

"Don't worry," I said. "I'm right there with you. There's something different about this one."

18

We didn't bother hanging around the crime scene any longer than needed. I had seen enough to know I had more questions than answers. Not a great way to solve a case. While copycats don't typically evolve, I worried our guy had. We now had five bodies and no solid leads. If our copycat really was another genius sicko, it didn't look good for the city.

Walking back to our car, I noticed the lookie loos were still standing in their driveways, whispering back and forth. Their hushed concerns said it all, though. They were terrified. They weren't used to having a homicide pop up in their backyard. Detroit had wormed its way into their safe little part of the world.

The press had also shown up. A swarm of them circled Wilkinson and me.

"Detective, what happened here? We heard there's been a double murder."

How do they get their information so damn fast?

"No comment," Wilkinson said flatly.

The same woman persisted. "Come on, detectives, tell us something."

I flashed a smile at the crowd before correcting the person that spoke. "It's agent, not detective."

"Agent? Why is the FBI involved? Are there any connections between what's happened here and the murder of Marian Ward?"

The questions came one after another. I stopped and turned to the female reporter. "We are helping the Grosse Pointe Police with the investigation. As of now there is no evidence to support a connection to the death of Mrs. Ward. That's all we have to say. Thank you."

Wilkinson leaned down toward me as we walked away. "You know we're not supposed to comment to the media."

"It's a bad habit I have," I said as I looked at him and waited for an answer.

He said nothing, just stared straight ahead and swatted at a fly.

The car chirped and my door unlocked. We had come to nickname our rental the Yellow Jacket. I had laughed when I first saw the yellow MINI Cooper. Now I thought we looked cool in it. As soon as we were out of sight of the press, I flipped the visor down to check my makeup.

Wilkinson looked over at me. "You look fine."

I did. I just wanted to hear it. And to break the tension.

After a few moments of silence, Wilkinson spoke. "The auto industry tie-in is our first real clue," he said.

"It's something to bite into."

"You think it matters that the victims work at different companies?"

"Nah. I'm assuming car execs in this town move around a lot."

"A few years ago, I saw a documentary about the city of Flint."

"Oh?" I asked just as I had a yawn attack. "Sorry. So this documentary…?"

Wilkinson gave me a quick look before he started. "Well, it was the late seventies. Pretty much everyone in Flint worked at the plants or made a living off the workers who worked there. Then GM started closing plants. The effect was disastrous. The entire town practically shut down. Everyone was suddenly out of a job. According to the film, the city never recovered."

An entire town? Someone living through that could develop a deep hatred for GM, maybe even all three of the biggies. I could see our guy being an ex-employee. What I couldn't quite accept yet was how a factory worker develops the chops to drain a body in seconds. Was he a hunter? I racked my brains trying to figure out if there were other angles. At the moment, disgruntled worker seemed to be a good way to go.

Wilkinson tapped the steering wheel. "What are you thinking? I hear grinding."

"I think we need to have a come to Jesus with the lieutenant about what the hell is going on here. Also, I think it'll be good to talk to the press."

"You just did."

"That's not the press I had in mind."

Wilkinson pulled into a park near the lake.

"What are you doing?" I asked.

"I thought we would swing by the area where the dead fisherman was found. This is Pier Park."

We turned into the parking lot. Half of the land jutting out from the shore was reserved for slips. The other half was a small park.

"Looks dead during the week," I said.

"Over there," Wilkinson pointed. "Near the far corner. They found the body inside that gazebo."

"From the looks of it, I'd say our killer had plenty of time with his victim."

19

By the time we had the car parked in the lot next to the precinct, the heat index had hit ninety-six degrees. The humidity didn't help either. It felt like I stepped out of an air-conditioned car and straight into a sauna. I fussed with my hair for a bit before noticing a newsstand on the corner. "Hang on. I'm going to grab a newspaper."

"A little light reading?" Wilkinson asked when I returned.

"You could say that." I flipped through the *Detroit Free Press* until I found the auto section. "This is who we need to talk to."

Wilkinson looked where I was pointing. "An auto industry columnist?"

"Who else would know everything there is to know about the auto industry? He might be able to help us narrow the field on our guy or point to an event worth investigating."

The second we opened the doors to the precinct, a whoosh of arctic wind swirled around us. It felt wonderful, but I slung my jacket back on. We were heading for the lieutenant's office, and he was the last person I wanted ogling my chest. Yes, I'm one of those women. If the wind blows, I become a pointer. It has its pros and cons.

Wilkinson stopped outside our office. "Tell you what; I'll get a head start on tracking this guy down. I'll rendezvous with you later."

"Okay. See you in a bit," I said and continued on.

I gave White's door a couple of knuckle raps.

"Agent Kane. Come inside." He motioned for me to sit. "What can I do for you?"

"I've got questions. I hope you have answers."

"Shoot away," he said as he leaned back in his chair and folded his hands over his lap.

"I had a conversation this morning with Michael Garrison—"

"I heard."

"Word travels fast around here."

White just looked at me blankly. I hoped his job wasn't to humor me. "He denies killing anybody except for a handful of hostages in the bank."

"Don't all inmates deny the charges against them?"

"Some of the hostages that day were shot. The rest were cut and bled to death. In my experience, serial killers don't change their M.O. on a whim. Perhaps over time, for some reason bearing significance."

"The two surviving victims said they saw Garrison shoot those people."

"Lieutenant White, I'm not arguing that. I believe Garrison shot a handful of hostages that day. It's the others I question. He has no medical knowledge or know-how that I'm aware of. Those incisions had to be precise and were done quickly."

"Agent Kane, everyone here appreciates your expertise with serial killers. You've got a record most in law enforcement would kill to have. But I have no idea why you're wasting time on a case that has already been put to bed."

I started to get irritated. White seemed like a nice guy and was probably toeing the line. Loyal cops do that; they get on board and roll with it. They don't question.

"Lieutenant, I also learned that the FBI agents that worked the Garrison case stopped the minute Detroit PD had him under arrest. Special Agent Tully said he received word from your department that the case was under control and their help was no longer needed."

"We had a handle on it. We were thankful for their help. What more is there to know? If they didn't close their cases properly, that's their problem and you should look to them for an answer."

"It just doesn't add up—Garrison going through the trouble of killing the hostages two different ways, confessing to all of the previous murders even though there's no evidence that I have seen so far that puts him at any of those crime scenes."

The lieutenant shifted in his seat. "Agent Kane, what is it you want from me?" he asked. His head had tilted down to one side. The crinkles in his forehead deepened. "What are you asking me?"

"I'm asking for the truth here."

"Truth?" His voice was noticeably lower. "Isn't that what we all want?" He clucked his tongue a bit. "The truth is what we believe. Do you believe the problems you have with the Garrison case will prevent you from catching the killer?"

"No."

White reached across the desk and took one of my hands, holding it gently between both of his. "If you catch the killer, Agent Kane, everything will work itself out."

Before he could let go of my hand I grabbed his. "Wait. What do you mean by that?"

White's eyes were glassy and tired. If there was something going on here, a cover-up, White probably knew about it. After looking me directly in the eyes for a few seconds, he seemed to relinquish the wall he had erected.

"I've worked for the Metro Detroit Police my entire life. I love this job. I believe we make a difference in this city. I'm a year away from retiring and collecting my pension. I've got a daughter who's getting married next spring and a wedding I need to pay for. I'm helping my son and his wife purchase their first home. I might not like what's going on here any more than you do, but I still need my job."

White leaned back in his chair and let out a heavy sigh. He was a defeated old man trying to make it to retirement.

"Can you—wait, strike that. Will you help me?" I asked, my voice low.

"I can't answer all your questions, but I'll try to help you as much as I can. You have got to understand the situation I am in, though."

I nodded. Hopefully, he understood the situation *I* was in.

20

"I was born to do this." That's what Chief Reginald Reed told others. He loved everything about law enforcement—everything except the visits.

They took place on the first Friday of every month at 9:00 a.m. sharp. For eight long years he had kept his displeasure about those trips to himself. He never spoke a word about his feelings to anybody, not even his wife. It was his little secret.

About quarter to nine in the morning, Reed would leave his office at Central and stroll over to the Coleman A. Young Municipal Center, formerly known as the City-County Building. Reed still called it that, and so did everyone else in Detroit that was his age. By 10:00 a.m. he would be done and could forget about it for four more weeks. That changed recently. He was now being summoned, at whim.

He received the call a little after eight that morning and was told to come over "A.S.A.P." no later than 9:30 a.m. Reed groaned a little. He hadn't even had his first cup of coffee, and he had already put up with some EMB—Early-Morning Bullshit.

Reed grabbed a cup of wake-up on the way out of the office, keen on downing it as quickly as possible. He liked being awake and having his senses on point for those meetings. It was important to know the difference between what was discussed and what was actually said.

Ten minutes later, Reed stood outside a drab building, a wall of gray with windows, really. *Functionality at its finest.* He drained the last of his coffee and tossed the cup into a trash bin. Walking toward the glass door, he used it as a mirror to look himself over and straighten his jacket.

As always, Steven Roscoe met Reed in the lobby. He had on his usual attire: a suit more aligned with a nightclub rather than the public sector. He extended his hand. "Good to see you, Chief. You keeping Detroit safe?"

Same fucking greeting every time. It had been that way from the very first visit. Reed never understood why he had to be escorted up to the office. It was ridiculous. Reed took the man's hand and shook it. "You still walking, ain't you?" It was his standard answer. Reed knew he wasn't really interested in an answer to his question.

Steven Roscoe told everyone he met to call him "Stevie." Thought it was catchier than Steven. Reed preferred to call him Weasel, on account of the way he looked, the way he acted, and the man he worked for. Either way, Stevie was slime poured into a suit. He walked with a swagger that left the taste of foulness in your mouth, and he always flashed that silly smile. You'd think he was running for office 24/7, the way he held himself up.

The ride up to the eleventh floor was quiet. The cordiality between the two never went further than the greeting downstairs. Stevie always led the way out of the elevator and down the hall to where the double wooden doors stood. He opened them and allowed Reed to enter before following and pulling them shut.

Sitting at a desk was the long-time administrative assistant to Stevie's boss, Louisa Sweeney. She looked up over her glasses with a wrinkle at the top of her nose before she recognized the man standing in front of her. "Reginald, how are you today?" She was the only person, besides his mother, who ever called him Reginald; most people called him Chief or "Yes, sir."

Reed smiled back and gave her a friendly squeeze to her arm. "I'm doing okay, Louisa. Thank you for asking."

"Is he ready to see us?" a voice piped up.

Louisa looked around Reed and saw Stevie behind him. Her smile disappeared. The crinkle on her nose resurfaced and it was business as usual. "Go on inside. He's waiting."

21

A well-dressed man sat behind a large mahogany desk with intricate carvings. He was puffing away on a cigar when Reed and Stevie entered the large office.

"You know it's against the law to smoke in this building," Reed said as he took a seat in front of the desk.

"I know that. I helped pass the law," the man said with a grin. A touch of gray detailed the sides of his slicked-back hair. Reed watched him pick up a crystal glass by the rim and dangle it. "Something to drink, a kick start for the day?" the man asked.

"I'm fine, thank you. How can I help you?"

"Why is Agent Kane investigating the old case and not the new one?"

"Your information is wrong. She's working the new case."

"That's not what I hear." The man took sip from the glass he held. He pursed his lips before swallowing the liquor. "I was informed she visited the jailhouse and spoke with Michael Garrison. After that, she spent time at the FBI field office looking at their case files."

"So she's getting up to date."

"Don't play me. It doesn't look like she's investigating the new murders."

"She's one of the best. I have complete confidence in her ability to apprehend our killer."

"Is that so?" The man stood up and walked over to a large window with sweeping views of the Detroit River. "Two more bodies showed up this morning. The press will be all over it."

"She's the best option we have right now. She'll catch him. You have my word."

The man turned around and brought a hand up to his chin, feigning deep thought. He looked Reed in the eyes. "Your word? Anything else you care to wager? Your career? Your life?"

22

Wilkinson and I returned to our hotel at ten that night. He pointed to the lounge. "You interested in a drink before heading up?"

That sounded great, but at the moment, I wanted nothing more than to change out of my grimy clothing and have a bath. Plus, Ryan and Lucy would be in bed soon. "I'm sorry." I pointed to my watch. "I want to catch the kids before bedtime."

Wilkinson flashed his dimpled smile. "I understand."

He had asked the same question every night since we had arrived in Detroit, and I had entertained it only once. I'd had fun. He told me all about his hippie parents and his Berkeley upbringing. He even mentioned his quick stint as a fitness model. I've yet to see Wilkinson with his shirt off, but his arms and shoulders did a wonderful job of backing up his claim. We were both buzzed when we finally headed upstairs that night. He kept sneaking peeks at me as we rode the elevator. I was glad he didn't make a move. I would have been too weak to resist, and he would have woken up in my bed the next morning.

I didn't doubt that we would have had fun, but we would be playing in a dangerous area. The truth was, we'd still have to work together. I wasn't quite ready to screw up our professional relationship should the morning after turn awkward. I admit I liked the attention. What woman wouldn't? Wilkinson was smart, funny at times, and dangerously good looking.

I returned his smile. "Tomorrow night, I promise."

"Goodnight, Abby."

He was also the only agent who called me Abby. I didn't mind that either.

When I got to my hotel room, I stripped off my holster and then my bra, leaving my blouse on. It was one of those days where the underwire killed. God, it felt good to let them breathe.

I made a beeline to the mini-bar and grabbed the bottle of Jameson. It wasn't the usual stock, so I had a bottle brought up the night I checked in. I poured a glass, neat, and sat on the bed with my back against the headboard. I let the first sip sit in my mouth for a second or two before swallowing. A few moments later, I felt the golden liquor working its way through my body. Calm had come to me. I took another sip, a larger one so I could savor that sweet taste. I started to think about the case but was able to banish it from my mind. I needed to relax. I had taken myself off duty.

A few sips later, I got off the bed and walked over to the window. The city was beautiful at night. The buildings reminded me of Hong Kong. Here I was, back in the thick of it, investigating a serial killer. And I was away from home. Even with me on East Coast time, I called the kids every night except for the few times Wilkinson and I worked past their bedtimes. I picked up my cell and dialed. I was looking to make good on my promise of being a mother to them.

• • •

Across the street from the hotel was an old office building. Most of the floors were vacant and dark. From the fourteenth floor, a person would have a clear view into Agent Kane's room if they wanted. And that's exactly what the stranger with the binoculars had hoped for. He had waited all evening for her return, and she did not disappoint. There she stood, wearing nothing but black panties and an unbuttoned blouse, unaware of her audience of one.

23

The next morning we took a drive out to Rochester Hills. Wilkinson had secured a half hour with Elliot Hardin, the auto columnist for the *Detroit Free Press*. We parked the Yellow Jacket in front of a two-story brick house.

"Looks like the reporting business pays well," I said, giving the neighborhood a once-over.

I rang the doorbell, which signaled the other doorbell. High-pitched yapping could be heard inside the house. I imagined the source to be small, brown, and ugly. A few seconds later, a tall, lanky fellow in a gray cardigan sweater answered the door. The tiny yapper stood between his legs, snarling. *You nailed it, Abby.*

"Mr. Hardin. I'm Agent Abby Kane and this is Agent Trey Wilkinson. We're with the FBI. My partner spoke to you earlier about answering a few questions."

The man seemed flustered, and his clothes were a bit disheveled. *What is it about writers that make them so messy?*

"Yes. Now I've got to tell you; I can only spare thirty minutes," he said.

"Mind if we come inside?"

"No, no, of course not." He held the door open and used his right leg to pin the dog against the wall behind him. "Be nice, Bella."

I slipped past the growling mutt and into the living room where Hardin motioned for us to sit. "Make yourselves comfortable. I'm going to put Bella out back."

From the looks of the décor, I was now assured he made more than a modest living. But that's not what was interesting about his place. Hardin's living room did double duty as a magnificent library. Hardcover, softcover, and leather bound editions lined shelves on every wall. A built-in hutch appeared to display his most prized novels. I recognized one of the books, Hemingway's *The Old Man and The Sea*.

"That's a first edition, first printing signed by the author himself," Hardin said as he returned to the room.

"So you're a book collector," I commented.

"Yes," he said as he looked around at the books and then back at me. "Have been my entire life." He took a seat opposite us. "Now, how can I help you two?"

"We're investigating the murders of Marian Ward and Dennis and Irene Walters."

"Yes, of course. Terrible thing to have happen to them. Any luck in catching the person responsible?"

"Well, that's why we've come to talk to you."

"Me?" Hardin straightened up in his chair and fiddled with his glasses. Surely you don't think I had anything to do with these murders."

"Quite the opposite, Mr.—"

Hardin waved his hand at me. "Please, call me Elliot."

"All right, Elliot. We're wondering, with your vast knowledge of the car industry, if anything comes to mind that could tie these two together, something that could have caused public outrage or angered workers or miffed the competition."

"You think the killer is after the auto industry?"

"We think there's a possibility he might be targeting auto executives."

Hardin leaned back in his chair and folded his hands on his lap. "What's in it for me?"

I looked at Wilkinson. He seemed just as confused. "I'm not sure what you're asking."

Hardin leaned forward and pushed his glasses back up his nose. "I'll come right out with it. I want the exclusive."

"Exclusive?" I didn't expect to hear that. Hardin wasn't that type of reporter. He maintained a column about the ins and outs of the big three automakers. He must have sensed our befuddlement.

"Let me explain," he said with a shake of his hand. "I've always wanted the big scoop, the front-page knockout. That doesn't happen too often in my area of focus, but a serial killer—"

"We didn't say there was a serial killer."

"Okay, a killer taking out auto execs one by one. Now that's front-page news."

"Tell you what; you don't print or mention anything until we catch our guy, and we'll give you the scoop… provided the information you give us helps us solve the case." I stuck my hand out. "Deal?"

"Deal."

Hardin went on to tell us how the GM plant shutdowns affected Flint. I had already heard the same story from Wilkinson. I hoped Hardin had more. "What does that have to do with our victims?"

"They both worked at GM at the time."

Now we're getting somewhere. "Are you telling us they were responsible for the plants shutting down?"

"Possibly…"

For a reporter, Hardin was light on his facts. "What does that mean?" I asked.

"I need to dig around before I can expand on that."

"Okay. Anything else you can tell us?"

Hardin leaned back and fiddled with his chin until he popped forward, clapping his hands together. "The local newspaper did a story on a man named Eddie Bass. Before the hard times hit, he championed GM, almost like their de facto mascot. He was known around town as The Motor. All he ever talked about was working at the factory, until he lost his job."

"I'm sure a lot of people had a beef with the company. Was there something special about him, besides being a cheerleader?"

"Well, I imagine he was shocked when they let him go. Probably found it difficult to deal with," Hardin said. "Granted he wasn't the only casualty, but a lot of people thought he would be safe, being who he was."

"Their number one fan," Wilkinson added.

Hardin nodded. "He didn't take it well. The story goes that he took to drinking and eventually drank himself to death. Left behind a little girl. His wife had died a few years after she was born. Cancer, I think."

"Where's the daughter now?"

"Before Eddie died, he and his daughter moved to Ohio to live with his sister. I'm guessing the sister ended up raising the kid after his death. You'll have to talk to her for more information."

We thanked Hardin, but I wasn't so sure we were any further along on the case.

24

That same morning, Katherine Carter drove her two boys to St. Mary's Grade School at the corner of Woodward and 12 Mile. Eight year-old Lorenzo was starting third grade. He was a pro at school and was excited to be back. Jackson, however, was starting kindergarten, and at four he had not grasped the concept of leaving his mom.

As soon as Katherine parked the white Land Rover in the school parking lot, Lorenzo got excited. "Mommy, Mommy, look. There's Marcus and Toby."

"Are you happy to see your friends again?"

"Yes! Yes!" Lorenzo had already unbuckled himself and gathered his things.

Katherine turned to Jackson. "What about you Mr. Big Boy? See how excited your brother is? It'll be fun."

Jackson sat in the back seat, pouting and wiping his eyes. "I don't wanna go."

"Come on, Jackson," his brother said. "You're going to love it."

Lorenzo ran ahead to meet his friends while Katherine carried Jackson to the drop-off point. She knelt down and faced Jackson toward her. She fixed his collar and straightened his Mickey Mouse backpack. "I know you're scared, but you're going to have a lot of fun, and your brother is here, too. Soon you'll have plenty of friends."

Katherine wiped away the tears that ran down Jackson's cheeks. It took everything she had not to cry herself as she struggled to maintain a smile. She wanted to hug him and take him home.

"He's going to be just fine, Mrs. Carter. We'll take good care of Jackson," one of the teachers said. Katherine watched the teacher lead Jackson away. He kept looking back at her with his puffy cheeks and big eyes. She turned away just in time to avoid him seeing her cry. A quick wipe before turning back to wave goodbye.

She hurried back to the SUV, her heels clicking noisily against the asphalt. Safely out of view, she let it out of her system. A few moments later, she composed herself and fixed her makeup. Katherine now had to go to work, the reason she wore an elegant black pantsuit that morning—certainly not the norm for most of the other stay-at-home mothers who were dropping off their children.

A twenty-five minute drive on Woodward Avenue had put Katherine just north of downtown Birmingham—Yuppieville. She turned off the main drag, down one of the tree-lined roads, until she found Hazelwood Street. Katherine parked two houses down from 813 Hazelwood, where a Victorian home with white and blue trim sat. It stood out from the other homes with their muted colors.

Katherine grabbed a handful of business cards from the glove box and slipped them into her purse. On her way to the house, she surveyed the neighborhood out of the corners of her eyes but kept her head straight. Katherine followed the cement path that cut through the lush front lawn and walked up the wooden steps. Just as she was about to knock, the door suddenly opened.

"Oh, excuse me," Katherine blurted, taking a step back.

The woman who opened the door jumped back as well. "Sheesh, you scared the heck out of me."

Katherine smiled at the woman. "I am so sorry. I was just about to knock. My name is Cheryl Newton. I'm a Realtor," she said, extending her hand.

The woman shook Katherine's hand. "Hi, I'm Rebecca Tanner. I'm sorry, but I'm on my way out."

Katherine looked behind the woman and saw two large suitcases. "I guess you're heading out of town?"

"My sister just had a baby, so I'm going to help out for a few weeks."

"Well now, that sounds like a lot of fun."

"I can't wait. It's her first. Mine are all grown and in college, so I'm the experienced one."

"Is your husband joining you?"

"No, he's busy with work right now."

Katherine dug into her purse and handed over her business card. "Well, I stopped by to see if you and your husband were having any thoughts on a lifestyle change."

"It's funny that you ask, because we were thinking of two things: either renovating or moving. We haven't decided yet."

"Well, when you're back in town, we can arrange a time to meet, and I can answer questions the two of you may have about selling and buying in this market. It might make that decision easier," Katherine said with a warm smile.

"That'll be nice."

"Oh, how silly of me." Katherine grabbed the door. "Let me hold this for you so you can get out."

Rebecca wheeled both suitcases out onto the porch.

"Give me one," Katherine motioned for Rebecca to hand her a suitcase. "I'll help you get this to your car."

"Oh, you don't need to do that."

"No, no, I insist." *It's the least I can do.*

25

Wilkinson and I buried ourselves back in the case files and worked to make sense of everything. It felt like we were walking in circles just gathering bits of information that led nowhere. I knew deep inside it all meant something; I just didn't know what. It was frustrating to say the least.

"Did those agents get back to you?" I asked.

"Not yet. I left messages though. I got a guy trying to track down a personal cell number. Might be able get a hold of them that way," Wilkinson said.

It seemed odd that we were having a difficult time locating fellow agents. *Were they avoiding us? If so, why?* I shook my head at the thought and picked up a file on another hostage from the Comerica heist. Just as I scanned the notes inside, it dawned on me; maybe we should follow up on the two survivors. I didn't recall coming across case files for them. "You find any files on the two surviving hostages?"

"Why?" Wilkinson asked. "You think they might know something about our current killer?"

"I'm curious to know if they'll corroborate Garrison's story."

"Why are you so bent on digging up the old case? There may be holes, but we're not here to find out why. We're here to catch the guy out there killing people."

I stood up and paced the room. "I know it doesn't make any sense, but my gut is telling me the two cases are connected. If Garrison is telling the truth, that he only shot people that day, then someone else in that bank cut those other people."

"And if Garrison is lying? We waste time and get nowhere."

I continued to dig around for those files but came up empty. *Another misplaced file?* I convinced Wilkinson to help, but the more we dug, the more it became apparent that what we were looking for didn't exist. I threw my arms up. "Nothing adds up. Files are missing. Cases aren't closed properly. This whole thing stinks of a cover-up." I tapped the desk. "Hey, assume Garrison is telling the truth, that he didn't kill everyone in the bank."

Wilkinson sighed. "Then your theory of another killer would be correct."

"Exactly."

"Maybe it was his girlfriend. Maybe she was slicing people up," he said, making a slashing move with is hand.

I shook my head. "Someone slit her neck. Why would Garrison kill his own girlfriend? Second, why use a knife and not the gun? Why kill people two different ways?"

"Because he's a pyscho."

"Normally, I would agree with you, but if my theory is right…"

Wilkinson paused for a moment, realizing his answer. "The original killer is still out there."

"And he could be killing again. This isn't a copycat. It's the same guy."

26

"That's crazy," Wilkinson said. "What about the surgical blade they found with Garrison's prints on it?"

"Planted."

"And the confession?"

"Coerced," I said. "It makes complete sense if you throw out any rational thinking."

"Why the cover-up then?"

"The citizens were scared, and the city felt pressured to capture this guy. So they latched onto Garrison and patched up the holes as best they could."

"Yeah, but wouldn't the real killer just keep on killing, proving they had the wrong guy?"

I leaned forward in my chair. "Not if, for some reason, luck played a role. Killer decides to stop for whatever reason at the same time. It totally works in the favor of the city. Everything is good for seven years and then there's a murder with the same M.O."

Wilkinson turned his palms up in front of him. "You know this sounds completely improbable."

"I know. That's why we had a roomful of scared police chiefs," I said pointing in the direction of the conference room. "They were stupid enough to go along with this idiotic plan. They can't come clean now. It would be political suicide."

Wilkinson rubbed his face and exhaled heavily. "The amount of people needed to make this cover-up work is huge. I'm not buying it."

"Doesn't matter if you buy it. The people of Detroit bought it a long time ago. Don't you see? We weren't brought here to catch a copycat. We were brought here to catch the original guy."

27

It all made complete sense to me, even if Wilkinson thought it was crazy. Sloppy casework, Garrison pleading innocence, White not wanting to talk—the real killer was never caught. It was all a farce. The people of Detroit were led to believe they were safe but, instead, were sold a security blanket littered with holes. It was only a matter of time before it fell apart.

Wrapping my head around the case made it ache. How many individuals were involved? How high up did it go? The chief of police? The mayor of Detroit? The governor of Michigan? The fallout would be devastating for many political careers. Was their failure to catch a killer over a five-year period so bad they had to orchestrate a cover-up of that proportion?

I didn't want to believe it, but it was a way to connect the dots. I prayed I was wrong, because I believed in the good of law enforcement. I prayed I was right, because that nut job needed to be put down.

My endorphins had kicked in. I practically kicked our office door down as I marched over to White's office. I stopped at his doorway with my sleeves rolled up and my hands planted firmly on my hips.

White looked at me for a moment before motioning for me to close his office door. He put aside his paperwork and watched me take a seat. I did my best to keep a level and professional tone. "Lieutenant White, I have one question for you, and I want an honest answer."

He nodded.

"Did the city of Detroit wrongly accuse and imprison Michael Garrison for the serial killings that took place before the Comerica robbery?"

White didn't move. He didn't flinch. He didn't look up to the left. He didn't roll his eyes. He didn't breath in or out heavily. He did nothing but look me straight in my eyes. "Agent Kane, are you sure you want to travel down this dark road?"

I couldn't believe that man had answered my question with a question. "That's not an answer," I said.

"Agent Kane, I'm going to try to say this as clearly as I can. This thing, it's bigger than both you and I, and it *doesn't* have anything to do with the guy out there killing folks."

The truth of the matter was the lieutenant was right. I could prove Garrison was innocent and the real killer was never caught, that it was a cover-up. And none of it would solve the current problem; someone was still killing innocent people.

"Lieutenant, if the person out there is the original killer, there's a good chance it could be one of the two hostages that survived."

"That's what we thought. We questioned the hell out of them. Nothing. We even watched them 24 hours a day, seven days a week, for six long months. We knew where they were at all times, what they were doing, who they spoke to, who their friends were. We even knew how many times they flushed their own toilet in a day. Neither one of them appeared to be the killer. Plus, the killings had stopped."

"So what happened?"

"The surveillance cost the city a fortune. We shut it down."

"With the current murders having the same M.O., didn't you guys think to check them out again?"

"It's not them, Agent. Trust me on this one."

My head ached more. If the killer wasn't one of the two hostages, then Garrison got lucky and shot the killer during his rampage, and the current killer really was a copycat.

"Agent Kane, we've already gone down this route. Forget about Garrison and the previous murders. Concentrate on the new ones and get this guy."

"Can I at least get the names of the surviving hostages?"

"I would say yes, but even I don't know who they are." White paused for a moment and rubbed his hand down his face, grabbing hold of his chin. "They were known around here as John and Jane Doe. It was that way from the very start. And if you're going to ask about the original surveillance team, there were three of them. Two were killed in the line of duty, and the other died of a heart attack."

"How convenient."

"It is, isn't it?" he responded flatly. The lieutenant leaned back in his chair. His eyelids looked heavy and tired. "Like I said, Agent, this is bigger than you and me both. Catch the killer and everything will be fine."

28

Wilkinson had just hung up his phone when I returned to our office. He had a super-sized smile on his face that enhanced his kissable dimples.

"Guess who I just spoke to?"

"Someone who can help us," I said, sitting against the desk.

"Michael Ton, the agent transferred to San Diego."

"What did he say?"

"Turns out he and the other agent were told by their superiors to cease all work on the case. Effective immediately, the FBI was no longer involved. They boxed it all up and filed it away."

"Anything else?"

Wilkinson looked down at his notes. "He said they thought it was strange that Garrison had confessed to all the murders. They personally found it hard to believe he was the guy. When they brought their concerns to their supervisor, Tully, they were quickly silenced. Soon after, they were transferred. And not by choice, either."

"That sucks. At least our fellow agents had the same thoughts as us about Garrison."

Wilkinson leaned back in his chair. "He sounded scared, Abby. He didn't want anyone to know we had spoken. He mentioned they might still be watching him."

"Who's they? The Bureau?"

"No, the City of Detroit."

White wasn't kidding. This was turning out to be huge. "Did he elaborate on that?"

"I prodded him but got nothing. He mentioned he still had a few friends in town, and he might be able to get names on those two surviving hostages."

I looked down at my watch. It was nearing 1:00 p.m. "Let's see if we can have another conversation with Garrison. He might be the only one who can identify those hostages."

As we drove over to the prison, I filled Wilkinson in on my conversation with the lieutenant.

"Bigger than both of us, John and Jane Doe… He said that?"

I nodded. "He's right."

"You're agreeing with him?"

"Solve the case and everything will be okay. He's right about that."

"Meaning if we catch our current killer, the cover-up won't matter. It'll be as if it never happened." Wilkinson shook his head. "This isn't how it's supposed to be."

Solve the case and go home, or stick our noses where they don't belong and end up like Agent Ton. Those seemed to be our options.

When we reached the prison a half hour later, the guard on duty told us we couldn't see Garrison. Didn't matter that we were FBI, or that he was part of an investigation, or that we had just interviewed him not long ago. We must have made enough of a commotion, because Gary Walczak showed up.

"Agent Kane, Agent Wilkinson. Good to see you two again."

I shook his hand and returned the smile. "Why can't we see Michael Garrison?"

Walczak reached around and huddled us in. "Look guys, I'm sorry to break the news to you, but inmate #04291144 is deceased."

Did I hear him right? Deceased? "Wait. You're telling us Michael Garrison, the guy we just questioned a week and a half ago, is dead?"

Walczak lifted his shoulders up and squinted. "I'm afraid so, guys."

Wilkinson had the same dumbfounded look on his face that I probably had on mine. Nothing could have prepared us for that.

"When? How?" Wilkinson asked.

"Just yesterday. He hung himself with his sheets."

I wonder how much help he had.

29

I won't lie and say that wasn't a blow to our investigation, but now wasn't the time to get hung up on Garrison's untimely death. As a concession, I asked Walczak if we could take a look around Garrison's cell. I hoped to find something that might help us.

"Normally that wouldn't be a problem," he said, "but it's already been cleaned out and his personal belongings have been boxed."

I flashed another smile at Walczak and grazed his arm with my fingertips. "Any chance we can take a look at that box?"

Walczak caved instantly and tripped over himself as he went to get the box.

"They teach you that move at the Academy?" Wilkinson asked as he mimicked my arm touch.

"You're so funny when you get jealous."

Wilkinson stuttered. "I—I'm not jealous. What makes you say that? Huh?"

I didn't respond, just continued looking straight ahead. I had won that little exchange.

Fifteen minutes later, we found ourselves in a tiny office with Walczak placing a box on a table.

"You got twenty minutes," he said before exiting.

Wilkinson grabbed the box and unloaded all of the contents onto a desk. "Looks like there's a bunch of writing, some drawings, a bible, a heavily used *Sports Illustrated* swimsuit edition—"

"Ewww," I said.

"Yeah, I'm not touching that either. Everything else appears to be junk." Wilkinson removed the writings and drawings and gave me half the pile. As I picked through my pile with the help of a pen, I realized most of Garrison's writing was incomprehensible—really a bunch of babble scribbled down. No glorious mantra or letter to an important someone, just a lot of repetitive writing of a couple of words.

"These drawings appear to be snapshots of what happened in the bank that day," Wilkinson said. "Look, these are bodies and that's a gun. This one has a knife. It's mostly the same visual drawn over and over."

I took a closer look. "Wait a minute." I grabbed the drawings from his hands and started to lay them out on the table. "They're numbered in the corner. These are drawn in the order the hostages were killed."

"You're right."

Wilkinson grabbed a pile and helped me organize the papers.

"So it looks like two women were the first to go," I said. "The word 'bank' is written next to them."

"Hold on; let me grab my notes." Wilkinson dug in a shoulder bag. "Okay, there were three bank tellers, and they were all women."

"Okay so the first to go were two of the tellers. This next drawing is of a dead guy with the word 'pizza' next to him."

"Okay, yes, one of the hostages was a teenager who delivered pizza."

Garrison had labeled each person based on what they did or what career they were dressed like. We already knew how they were killed, but now Garrison had provided us with an order.

"So, let's run through this again." Wilkinson counted off with his fingers. "First to go were the two bank tellers, then the pizza delivery kid, the librarian and security guard were next, then the old lady and two of the businessmen, his girlfriend, the trainer, the construction guy, another teller, the bank manager, and lastly, the third businessman." Wilkinson added the order in which they were killed to his notes. "His girlfriend was the last person to die by a knife. Every person after that was shot."

I shifted my weight. "Okay, so the killer finally gets the girlfriend. That sets Garrison off and he proceeds to kill everyone, hoping he kills the one who did it. So we know all the people killed before his girlfriend couldn't be the killer. It has to be one of the last seven hostages." *He told us the truth.* "We should be short two bodies since there were two survivors." I counted the bodies in the drawings. "Yep, we're short two."

"And of course there are no case files on our John and Jane Doe," Wilkinson added.

"If what Lieutenant White said was true, with the surveillance coming up empty, Garrison most likely shot the real killer," I said.

"It seems that way."

"Wait a minute." I flipped through Garrison's writings until I came to a page with the same thing written over and over. "I think we have another clue." I showed it to Wilkinson.

"The Professor and The Student," he said.

"Garrison seemed obsessed with these two."

Wilkinson ran his index finger back and forth across his chin. "So the surviving hostages were a professor and a student."

"Maybe. He seemed obsessed with the two labels."

"And you said Lieutenant White had surveillance on both parties, and nothing came out of it."

"He did say that, but there's no evidence of that being true either, because there are no files on it."

My partner shook his head and threw his head back. "So our killer could be a professor or a student, male or female, or Garrison could really have shot the killer." Wilkinson threw his hands up into the air. "Well, that's considerable progress made."

I didn't blame Wilkinson for being frustrated. It seemed as though every step forward we took, we got knocked back a mile. But for some reason, I still believed Garrison. Over time, I think he had started to doubt the killer was the businessman and suspected it could have been one of the two surviving hostages. He could only have been sure if he killed everyone. Thinking about this day and night must have driven him crazy.

30

Everybody knew Stevie Roscoe. Born and raised in Detroit, he grew up in the same Brush Park project housing as Diana Ross and Smokey Robinson. He may not have been blessed with a golden voice, but Stevie had something just as moving, the gift of gab. He could talk anybody, even a person he had just met, into doing something for him. The story on Stevie was that he could talk the archbishop of Detroit into skimming donations and handing it over to him, if he wanted. He did.

He was charming. That was his talent—the ability to make people around him carry out his will, none of it good. Morally corrupt doesn't even start to shed a light on how blackened his soul was.

Stevie walked into the lobby of the City-County Building a little before eight every morning and smiled at every person he passed. He would always follow that up with a, "How you doin'?" or a, "Lookin' good." He didn't care much about their response.

He would then enter the elevator and ride it up to the eleventh floor alone—the way he preferred it. A finger point with a smile was how he always addressed the administrative assistant, Louisa Sweeney. She never paid him any attention—the only one to ever get away with it.

Closing the door behind him, Stevie would then take a seat in the same chair he had sat in for the last twelve years and wait patiently. That day, his mind drifted, and Stevie was lost in dreamland when a booming voice yanked him back to reality.

"Stevie!" The gentleman behind the desk called out. He was off the phone and looking straight at him. "What's this fucking bullshit I hear about that agent trying to talk to Garrison again?"

"It's been dealt with."

"What the fuck do you mean by 'dealt with'? Don't give me some bullshit story now." The man followed with a finger point and a raised eyebrow.

Stevie smiled. "I ain't never let you down and I ain't about to. Garrison won't be a problem, and that's all you need to know."

"I keep hearing whisperings in my ear that she's investigating the old case."

"That I won't lie about. She's a tenacious little bitch." Stevie stood up and walked over to the wet bar. "Scotch?" His boss nodded and Stevie poured two glasses.

"How close is she to catching the copycat?"

"From what I hear, she's making progress. The problem is, she's also making progress on the old case."

"What about the other agent?"

"He ain't no worry. That girl's the brain of the bunch. We misunderstood her diligence and stubbornness. I'm making a few changes." Stevie handed a glass to his boss.

"Who's watching her?"

"I am now. Have been for a while."

"Good. I know I don't have to tell you how important it is that nothing gets out. I want you to get rid of everything having to do with the old case. Should have done it years ago."

"I'll personally take care of it." Stevie grinned and took a sip of his drink.

The man sitting on the other side of the desk put his glass down and leaned forward. His eyes narrowed. "Don't fuck this up, Stevie. You've got to contain this bullshit because if it gets out and comes back to me, I'mma take every muthafucker involved down with me. You got that?"

Stevie nodded and wiped his palms on his pants. Time to tighten the screws. A lot of people didn't like Stevie; some even feared him, and rightfully so. As chief of staff, he had a lot of power. But even Stevie himself feared someone. And that was Leon Briggs, mayor of Detroit.

31

The tiny bar located at the back of the strip mall was near closing when the front door flew open and out walked a boisterous Rick Tanner. GM's chief engineer loved one thing more than cars, and that was variety. With his wife out of town visiting her sister and her newborn, Rick indulged.

Hanging on his arm was a giggling brunette, dressed in a short black dress with heels to match. She cooed over him as he openly pawed at her. *When the cat's away, the mice will play*, he thought.

Rochester Hills was two towns over from Birmingham, far from his neighborhood. Rick preferred it that way. He enjoyed the anonymity it afforded him. It made it easier to drag a bar babe home without having to worry about whether anyone was watching him.

Tonight someone *was* watching.

Preston Carter observed the couple from his silver Mercedes. Their playful grabbing, the light kissing... His wife was doing a wonderful job with Rick the Prick. Preston couldn't help but give him a nickname; the man was, after all, groping his wife.

The two made their way across the parking lot, got inside a black Cadillac Escalade, and drove off. Preston started his engine and followed the SUV. He wasn't in any hurry and didn't bother to keep up. He knew exactly where they were going. By the time he put his car in park and turned off his lights, the happy-go-lucky couple had already exited the Escalade parked in the driveway of the blue and white Victorian.

Parked under a large maple tree, Preston sat unnoticed in the vehicle, patiently tapping his fingers against the leather steering wheel while he hummed. He kept checking his cell phone like a teenage girl. Close to an hour had passed before his phone finally beeped.

"I'm ready for you," the text message read.

Preston exited the vehicle and stuck to the shadows as he moved across the street. A tingling sensation overcame his body as he closed in on the house. Within seconds he stood on the porch and reached for the door handle. He quietly let himself in, gently closing the door behind him. He could hear moaning—a man's voice. His footsteps were muffled as he made his way up the carpeted stairs. With each step, his chest tightened, making him even more aware of his beating heart. He loved the lead-up; it was almost as exciting as the act itself.

Down the hall he moved, toward the room where he heard moaning. He pushed the master bedroom door open. There was his beautiful wife, naked except for her heels and latex gloves. She reached for her dress on the floor.

"Don't," Preston said. "Stay the way you are. I love it."

Katherine returned a devilish smile to her husband while waving her finger at him. Preston walked over to her and kissed her on the lips while he reached around to her behind and gripped a cheek in each hand and squeezed. His penis grew erect. "I want you," he whispered.

"You can have me when we're done here," she answered.

Preston kissed his wife once more before looking over to the bed, where an unconscious Ricky Pricky lay naked and tied up. "He doesn't appear to be excited."

Katherine looked at Rick's genitals. "Hmm, he showed signs earlier. I guess the scalping turned him off." She laughed.

The top of Rick's head was a bald, bloody mess. It wasn't enough to kill him, but it appeared to be awfully painful. Preston reached inside of his jacket and removed his own set of latex gloves and a fresh scalpel. He snapped them on and removed the safety cap from the tiny but deadly blade.

Earlier, Rick Tanner had no clue how grim his situation had become when he brought home the woman from the bar. Even when he let her strip him down and tie him up, he was having a jolly time. She had squatted over his face and teased him, staying just out of reach of his lickity-licks. He had been so enamored by the view, he hadn't noticed her smile had disappeared. He only whined and begged her to return when she left her perch.

She'd removed a pair of beige latex gloves from her purse and then a ball gag that she had slipped over his head, gently. At the same time, she gripped his erection lightly. He wasn't thrilled about the gag, but how could he resist? She had his cock in her hand. He played along. Nothing to worry about. Harmless fun. Why, it wasn't long ago that he had the best view in the house. What threat could the woman pose? They were playing a game, right?

Nothing could have prepared him for what happened next. She raised her hand and revealed a small surgical blade. Rick's eyes widened; so did Katherine's smile. She quickly jumped up onto the bed and plopped herself down on his chest, forcing the air from his lungs. Even though he struggled to catch his breath, he never lost sight of the threat in her hand. She slid up and down his chest and moaned.

What the hell is going on? he thought. Before he knew it, she had placed the blade against the side of his head.

Katherine looked down at Rick and realized she didn't really need the gag. Rick Tanner appeared to be a crier, not a screamer. She then proceeded to cut into the flesh along his head. It wasn't long before she held his scalp in front of him for his viewing pleasure. He screamed and she giggled. Finally she had leaned in and whispered into his ear. "Do I still turn you on?"

"Wake up!" Preston called out, slapping the unconscious man in the face.

Rick opened his eyes and blinked repeatedly until he could focus on the man sitting at the foot of the bed. To see another blade set loose the tears, accompanied by muffled moaning. The more he cried, the more he bled. Boohoo.

Preston scooted closer to the head of the bed. He grabbed hold of Rick's inner thigh and nicked the femoral artery. The instant eruption of thick red left a spattering of tiny dots on Preston's face. He continued with the other leg. Rick screamed uncontrollably when he saw the mini geyser of life spurting from both legs.

Preston grabbed Rick by the face, forcing the man to look him straight in the eyes. He leaned in close, his stare never wavering. He brought the scalpel up and held it off to the side. Rick's eyes darted to the blade, but Preston yanked on his head to bring his focus back. He wanted to see the terror in Rick's eyes when he opened up the prick's neck.

32

The early morning rain had brought some temporary relief to the punishing heat; finally, a day where I wasn't perspiring like a man. Unfortunately, it didn't bring any relief to our jobs. We were back in the town of Birmingham for the same reason we were first brought here.

A young uniform from Birmingham Police escorted Wilkinson and me inside the residence at 813 Hazelwood. We were told Detectives Solis and Madero were already upstairs in the master bedroom, looking over the body. We maneuvered around a crime scene investigator on the steps, dusting for prints, and headed on up.

Right off the bat, I noticed similarities with Marian Ward's crime scene. Both victims were tied to the bed and gagged. Both were found in blood-soaked sheets.

"Let me guess—three incisions?"

Detective Solis spun around followed by Detective Madero.

"Very observant, Agent," Madero snickered.

I completely ignored him. Sometimes I meet people I just don't get along with and never will. Madero was proving to be one of them. I'm sure the feeling was mutual.

"He's also missing a scalp," Solis added.

I walked over to the bed. It looked like someone had placed a rice bowl on his head for a guide. Did scalping the victim mean anything? Was our killer trying to communicate with us? None of the other auto executives had that done to them. Rick Tanner and Marian Ward were both tied and gagged. Dennis Walker, along with his wife, had been staged in their vehicle, though I suspect the wife was collateral damage. Why the sudden change in his ways? Was our guy bored?

Wilkinson joined me near the bed. "Everything appears to be the same except for the scalping."

I whispered, "Wait a minute. Wasn't one of the hostages at the Comercia robbery scalped?"

"You're right. I remember coming across that information."

I looked back at Solis. "Does he work for one of the big three?"

"Yeah," Solis said. "Rick Tanner. He was a top engineer at GM."

"That's not good."

"Yeah, our killer is definitely targeting car guys." Solis flipped through his notepad. "He's married. We're still trying to track down the wife, but I doubt she did this."

I agreed. "It's not her."

"I wonder if our guy is progressing, switching it up." Wilkinson said.

Solis turned to him. "Could be. Maybe we're closer to him than we think, and he's trying to throw us off track."

I motioned to the various techs. "Could everyone in the room clear out for a few minutes with the exception of Detective Solis and Detective Madero? Thank you."

I waited until the last person had exited the room before closing the door. I then brought the two detectives up to date on our theory that the original killer was never caught and was the one killing again. I had to take a chance that they were not involved in the cover-up. I needed people on our side we could trust.

From the dumbfounded looks on their faces, it appeared my gamble had paid off.

"Are you sure? A cover-up, dirty cops?" Solis shook his head.

Madero stared at the carpet. "That means we're ruling out the wife?"

I acknowledged Madero with a nod. "I would still follow up, though. Also, one of the victims from the Comerica robbery was scalped. I don't believe that information was public."

Madero started to mutter. Solis couldn't stop tugging at his collar. I hoped I wasn't losing them.

"It's crazy. I know that. But it's not implausible. The information connects the dots. Nothing else we've explored has led anywhere."

Solis placed his hands on his hips. "Okay, say this is all true. What do we do?"

"First off, we keep this to ourselves. We continue to work the case like it's a copycat, knowing we're after the original killer. The two of you need to familiarize yourselves with the old cases. These new kills are just a continuation from the past. Talk to the neighbors. Someone had to have seen something. And check out the local sex shops. See if we can get the names of everyone who's recently bought an orange ball gag."

33

The first recognizable sign was an overbearing, metallic smell. The second sign was unavoidable. The crimson substance was everywhere: pooled on the patio tiles, dripping from the tables and chairs, soaked into the lawn, and smeared inside the bounce house. In some of the areas where multiple bodies congregated, the puddles were still splash-worthy.

Preston sat quietly on the patio chair, admiring his handiwork. A total of twenty-two bodies lay strewn about the backyard. Blood dotted Preston's face and clothing. The grin on his face still stretched from one side to the other.

He had finished them all off, starting with the parents. From there, he moved on to the fourteen children. They were easy—surprisingly, even his own. The last to go was his wife. He still held onto the scalpel he used. In his other hand, he gripped his wife's hair, holding her head up. Her neck had been opened from one end clear across to the other side. Blood still dripped onto the cement. It was the only sound, except for the buzzing of flies.

A scream woke Preston up from his dreamy haze.

"Help!" a little girl shouted. She was in the grasps of the Tickle Lady who tickled her victims until they screamed mercy. It was Lorenzo's birthday. The Carters were celebrating. And everybody was still very much alive.

Fourteen boys and girls high on sweet stuff were running, screaming, laughing, shouting, and crying. Fueling that revelry was a clown making larger-than-life balloon animals. There was also a face painter hard at work, turning children into dogs and cats and zombies. Four kids were flipping and flopping their brains out in the castle-shaped bounce house. Spread out amidst the chaos were carts serving hotdogs, pizza, popcorn, and ice cream. Colorful balloon bouquets dotted the yard, while a criss-cross of paper streamers hung above.

The children weren't the only ones enjoying themselves. The parents had gathered around a few tables and were content to chit-chat and dine on this same child-friendly diet. Preston graciously mingled with each guest while his wife played the perfect host, ensuring no wine glass went empty.

Before heading back into the house to fetch a lighter, Katherine signaled to her husband.

Preston put two fingers into his mouth and let out the whistle of all whistles, gaining the attention of every moving body.

"Gather around," Preston called out as he walked over to the cake table. "It's time to sing *Happy Birthday*."

The cake itself was an elaborate creation spanning twenty by thirty inches. A detailed carousel sat in the center, while a roller coaster ran along the borders. There was also a balloon vendor, game booths, and a cotton-candy maker. It was the perfect amusement park scene, except all of the people were zombies, Lorenzo's current fascination. Katherine had caved on the cake but held firm on not turning their backyard into a graveyard.

She lit eight candles. Lorenzo took a front and center position and, with much anticipation, clapped like a seal. Preston started the singing with a hum from his baritone voice. He flailed his arms like an amateur conductor, encouraging everyone to join in. When the crowd hit their last note, Lorenzo let out a huge breath of air, extinguishing the candles. A second later, they flickered back to life, forcing him to try again and again. The joke candles were a big laugh for everyone, including Lorenzo. Katherine and another mother doled out plates of cake and ice cream to the mob of sugar-crazed children.

Later, Preston followed his wife into the house, where he watched her return a bucket of ice cream to the freezer. His groin tingled as he approached her.

"The party's a hit. You did a wonderful job, dear," he said as he spun his wife around and kissed her.

"I'll have to agree with you on that," she said playfully.

"Anything else planned?"

"Nope. The cutting of the cake was the last thing to do." She looked at her watch. "The entertainers have an hour left on their booking. We should be good to wrap things up then."

"That sounds great, but I'm wondering if you had anything planned for me." Preston flashed his wife a diabolical smile and lowered his voice. "The urge is there," he said. It had only been a week since the Tanner kill, but Preston was hungry again.

"I do, dear. Be patient. I have a few kinks to work out and then my sweetie can have fun. Terrible fun."

34

A full day of poring through case files would turn anyone's brain into dead matter. Wilkinson and I were beat. We needed a break. That meant steaks and a couple bottles of good wine. White recommended the London Chop House, a Detroit legend, only a few blocks from the station. We wasted very little time with the wine list and ordered a bottle of red.

"To the Bureau," Wilkinson said as he raised his glass.

I tinged my glass against his and smiled. We were well into our second glasses. It was full of flavor, bold and very yummy—perfect for the aged rib eyes we had just ordered. I was having a nice time. I kicked off a heel and playfully kicked at Wilkinson's foot.

"Someone let her guard down and decided to relax," he said, smiling.

"Maybe it's time I relax, Wilky." I wasn't sure what I was doing or where it was going. All I knew was we got along really well, and he looked dreamy.

He reached over and clinked his glass against mine. "I'll drink to that."

I kicked off my other heel and tag teamed him while I wondered out loud, "Sure could use a foot massage…"

Wilkinson laughed. "If you finish all of your dinner, we'll see about a massage."

Wilkinson's constant eye contact made me giggle and feel lightness in my chest. I suddenly wished we weren't sitting on opposite sides of the table.

"How's the family handling you being away?" he asked.

Before I could answer, my phone started to buzz. *Damn!* I took a peek and smiled. "Speaking of family." Lucy had sent me a text. "Can I stay up?" I texted her back to go to sleep and I would talk to her tomorrow. I looked back at Wilkinson, who hadn't stopped smiling. "It's the little one, Lucy. Ever since I taught her to text, it's been nonstop."

"Must be tough."

"It is. I want to be there for them. This is Lucy's first year in an American school, kindergarten. Every day is an adventure for her. It's so fun to hear her talk about what she's learned."

"What about the older one? Is he handling the change well?"

I nodded my head as I tilted my wine glass against my mouth. "Oh, he's acclimated fast. He's in the third grade so school's not a big deal. He loves the city and has a few friends in the neighborhood. I've got nothing to worry about with him."

"That's great to hear."

"Po Po on the other hand," I tilted my head from side to side, "she's something else. I know she means well, though."

"What about Hong Kong?"

"Hong Kong I don't miss. There's nothing there for me."

"What about your folks?"

"They moved north to the city of Harbin years ago after my father retired. He thought it would be great to run the big ice festival the city puts on every year."

Wilkinson topped off both our glasses. "You ever thought of doing something else?"

What, like marry you and move to the south of France where we can frolic naked in the countryside? "All the time," I chuckled as I raised my glass. "Here's to figuring that out."

No sooner had I taken a sip than my phone went off again. That time it was a call.

"Agent Kane, here."

"Agent. It's Elliot Hardin."

I mouthed the columnist's name to Wilkinson.

"Mr. Hardin. I didn't recognize the number."

"I'm calling you on one of those disposable phones. I have reason to believe I'm being watched."

"Why? What happened?"

"Let's just say digging around has stirred up the nest. I think someone broke into my house the other day, and a strange car sat in front of the house all night."

"Did you report it?"

"Don't worry about me, Agent. Listen, I don't have much time. I have some information for you."

"What is it?"

"Not over the phone. Tomorrow. Meet me at the Coney Island on Fourteen and Maple. Nine o'clock sharp. Don't be late."

Before I could say anything, Hardin hung up.

"What?"

"Whatever it is, we'll have to wait until tomorrow."

Our steaks came soon after. We tried to salvage the evening, but the call had put both our minds back into work mode. We'd had a fire going, and Hardin had come by and pissed on it.

35

The next morning, we arrived at the Coney Island at nine sharp, just as Hardin had instructed. I spotted him in a booth at the back of the restaurant, chewing on his nails. He looked scared and like he hadn't slept much.

I slid into the seat opposite him, and Wilkinson swung a chair around and sat at the opening of the booth.

"Can I get you two something?" a waitress asked.

"Coffee for me. Hot water for her, please," Wilkinson answered.

I pulled out a little tin that held my loose leaf tea and set it on the table.

Hardin had a good growth on his face and smelled like he could use a shower.

"What's going on? Earlier you said someone was following you."

"I don't have much time. Back in the eighties there was a young group of executives at GM—hotshot up-and-comers. From what I understand, they secretly formed a pact and became very influential in the company. There were rumors about them, but nobody knew who they were."

"A secret pact?"

"Yes, they called themselves the Redline Rogues or RRs."

"Elliot, I don't understand," I said, shaking my head. "How does this tie in to our investigation?"

"The plant closures that took place in Flint were all because of the RRs."

The waitress returned to our table and placed two cups down on the table. We barely noticed. "Yeah, and…?"

Hardin clapped his hands together. "Closing plants is an unpopular thing to do. It's not the first thing that a company thinks of when they need to save some money."

"But that's part of doing business, right?" I still didn't see the importance of what Hardin said.

"Yes. But the RRs, they championed the project. They pushed for it. They convinced the heads of GM at the time that it was in the company's best interest."

I sat back, wanting to hear more. "How?"

Hardin shrugged. "That I don't know, but you can imagine this might piss a person off."

I glanced at Wilkinson but couldn't tell if he bought the story. "What happened to the RRs?" I asked.

"They supposedly went on to have great careers. It was about personal gain. I wouldn't be surprised if some other folks outside of the group benefited as well."

"How big was this group of RRs?"

"There were six." Hardin gave the restaurant another quick look. "I have to go."

"Wait. Were any of them our victims?"

"I'm out of time." Hardin stood up. He removed a piece of paper from his shirt pocket and placed it on the table. "I'll text you the others when I have them," he said over his shoulder as he moved toward the door.

I picked up the paper. There were four names written down.

Wilkinson eyed the paper as he sipped his coffee. "What does it say?"

"There are four names. Three are our victims. The other one is Archie Becker."

"You believe him?" he asked.

"Right now, I don't know what to believe. This whole case is getting stranger by the minute."

I put a call into Solis and Madero and filled them in. I wanted them to track down Archie Becker for questioning and put a patrol car on his residence. For all we knew, the killer could have been targeting him as we spoke.

36

With Hardin admitting he was being watched, I had to assume we were, too. Whoever was responsible for the cover-up was eager to make sure it remained that way. It seemed like every person we came in contact with didn't want to talk or appeared to be scared of something.

With the revelation of the Redline Rogues, Eddie Bass' sister, Claire, quickly became a person of interest. I somehow had a hunch "The Motor" might have known about them. And if he did, my hope was that he had mentioned them to Claire or his daughter. I was glad Hardin had emailed me Claire's address the day after we met.

The drive down to Mansfield, Ohio took us a little less than three hours. We were told she lived by herself just outside of the city in an old farmhouse.

When we arrived, the structure looked a lot older than I'd pictured. It was quaint and cozy, and the wood had that aged look that's all the rage for country living in the Hamptons. Still, I wished I had a hard hat for entering.

Wilkinson parked the Yellow Jacket near the front of the house. Besides a few chickens pecking around, there didn't seem to be any other signs of life—no noises coming from or around the house. Claire lived off the highway at the end of a quarter-mile dirt road. She had no neighbors.

The screen door rattled when I knocked on it. Wilkinson tried peeking inside through one of the windows. That's when we heard the voice behind us.

"Can I help you two?"

We turned to face an elderly woman dressed in jeans and a red flannel shirt. She wore a wide-brimmed hat and had a blue and white handkerchief tied around her neck. But the 12-gauge shotgun in her hands was what really caught my attention.

"Easy, lady," Wilkinson said.

"Claire Bass?" I asked.

"Yes, that's me," she responded, calmly and without waver. Her eyes were squinted and her finger was wrapped around the trigger.

"We're FBI agents. You're not in trouble. We just want to ask you a few questions."

She remained quiet and focused.

"We're going to reach into our jackets and take out our IDs, okay?" I said.

She kept a close eye on both of us. Her arm seemed to be shaking a little. Either the gun was getting heavy, or it was some uncontrollable tic. I didn't want to find out. She took a few steps closer and leaned forward, examining our identification.

Satisfied, she lowered the gun. "I'm sorry about that, but I live alone and I'm old. I've got to be careful."

"We understand," I said. "You snuck up on us there."

Claire chuckled a little. "It's a good skill to have." She stomped her shoes on a worn mat before entering the house. "Make yourself at home while I put a pot of coffee on."

It was impossible to ignore the décor. The inside of Claire's house was neatly cluttered with little Hummel figurines. Where there was space, there was a little boy or girl carrying a bucket of water, praying, or picking flowers.

Fifteen minutes later, Claire shuffled back into the living room with three mugs and placed them on the coffee table. She appeared to be in her sixties and able, though she didn't stand fully upright. "Any of you take cream or sugar with your coffee?" she asked, pausing in front of her rocking chair.

We both shook our heads and watched her sit and slowly start to rock.

I spoke first. "Claire, I'm Agent Abby Kane and this is Agent Trey Wilkinson. We're investigating a series of murders that have taken place in Detroit—"

"Wasn't me," she shot back.

I gave Wilkinson a quick look before speaking. "We're aware of that. We're here to talk about your brother, Eddie Bass."

"He's dead. So it wasn't him, either."

I smiled. "We're aware of that, too. We understand your brother was a vocal supporter of GM while he worked there."

"They called him The Motor. He loved working for that company. Being able to make a living and provide for his family made him a proud man. Terrible thing they did to him."

"You mean the company, right?"

"Who else would I be talking about, dear? Not only him, but the whole town got hit."

"That's when he moved here, with his daughter?" I asked.

"Yes. His wife, Christine, had already passed. She had breast cancer. There wasn't any need to stay in that town. It had a terrible effect on him. He started drinking... I worried about him."

"So he moved here, to Ohio?"

"I finally convinced the stubborn mule." Claire drifted off into her thoughts before speaking again. "He had only been here for a little over a year when he passed." Claire continued to rock and sip. Her eyes appeared heavy, but she never kept them off of us for long.

"Claire, did Eddie ever talk about the Redline Rogues?"

She took a moment before answering. "Not that I recall. What is it?"

"A bunch of GM executives. There's a rumor that they were responsible for shutting down the plant in Flint." I figured it was best to leave out their names and the fact that three of them were dead.

"Oh, you're talking about the Good Boys," she said. "That's what Eddie called them. Anyhow, he came upon them late one night at the plant, had forgotten something in his locker. That's when he overheard a group of people talking in hushed tones."

"Did he know them?" I asked.

Claire shook her head. "No, but he snuck up on 'em and listened. He said he only heard bits and pieces. He had a bad ear," she motioned, "but he swore they were talking about shutting down the plant. Eddie was the one to spread the word before the company said anything. Everyone thought it was crazy talk until it happened."

Claire's story supported what Hardin told us earlier. Pieces were coming together. I started to believe our own hype; someone wanted revenge for what the RRs did.

"Did Eddie mention what they looked like?"

"From where he hid, he said he couldn't see them all too well. But he was sure there were men and women. As far as I know, he never told anyone where he got his information on the plant closing. If you ask me, I'd say something had him spooked."

I looked around but saw no pictures of him or his daughter.

"What about Eddie's daughter? Do you think he mentioned it to her?"

"You mean Lisa?" Claire shrugged and took another sip of her coffee.

Wilkinson wrote her name down in his notepad.

"Sorry, we didn't have a name for her. Do you know where we can find her?" he asked.

"I don't know where she is. We never did see eye to eye. She moved out when she was seventeen."

"Do you have an address or a phone number?"

Claire finished the last of her coffee. She stood up and cleared our cups on the way back to the kitchen. I looked at Wilkinson. "Looks like our chat is over."

"No address or number. She could be anywhere," he said.

I tried to remain optimistic.

Claire reemerged from the kitchen with a dishcloth in her hand. Wilkinson and I both stood up.

"Do you have any idea how we can get a hold of Lisa? It's very important we talk with her."

"You think she killed those people?"

"No, not all," I said. "We're just trying to gather as much information as possible."

"She was a quiet one. Was cordial to most. She didn't have me fooled, though. That girl had a mean streak that would surface every now and then."

"In what way?"

"The littlest things would set her off. I rearranged her closet once. I never did *that* again." Claire bent down and gave the coffee table a once over. She then walked over to a desk and wrote something down.

"You might try Flint. It's where she's from," she said as she opened the front door. She slipped me a paper with a name and an address on it as we exited the house.

37

We were still an hour's drive from Detroit when I got a call from Solis. I was expecting an update on Archie Becker, the suspected RR. What I got instead felt like a punch to the gut.

"I hope you're sitting down."

"Spit it out," I said.

"Your reporter friend, Elliot Hardin. He's dead."

"Come again?"

"Couple of hunters came across his car in the woods. He was inside with a gunshot wound to the back of his head."

I whispered to Wilkinson that Hardin was dead.

"There were two vehicle tracks, so whoever did this was in the car with him with an accomplice following."

"Why do you think that?"

"Well, the only reason to come up here is to hunt elk, and Hardin doesn't look the type."

I shook my head slowly. Hardin had been telling the truth earlier. *How the hell am I supposed to solve this case if my informants keep showing up dead?*

"What about Becker?"

"We tracked him down at Ford. He's one of their top engineers. He denies knowing anything about the RR. He's also refusing any help from the police. We put a patrol car outside his house anyway, as a visual deterrent in case our guy is targeting him. He's not being helpful, though."

"Keep an eye on him until we can get back. I want to question him personally."

38

We reached Archie Becker's house a little before seven that night. The sun had started to set, but kids of all ages were still out playing. Becker lived alone in the family-friendly Bloomfield Hills, north of Birmingham. Solis and Madero were parked out front in a brown unmarked vehicle waiting for us. Across the street was a patrol car, like they said.

When I got closer to their car, the detectives exited. "We followed him back from work," Solis said. "He's been home for maybe forty minutes."

"Thanks. Wait outside, please."

Wilkinson and I continued up the driveway of the ranch style home. We rang the doorbell.

A neatly dressed man answered the door. His posture deflated when he saw us. "How can I help you?" he asked, dryly.

"Archie Becker? I'm Agent Kane. This is Agent Wilkinson. We were hoping we could ask you a few questions."

Becker flopped his head to the side and exhaled loudly. "Look, Agents. I've already answered a bunch from the two sitting in the car." He pointed.

"I realize that, Mr. Becker, but you didn't answer our questions."

He let out another breath of air and added an eye roll. His antics were starting to annoy me.

"I suppose you want something to drink," he said as he swung the front door open and led the way.

Actually, I would love to punch some sense into you.

Wilkinson and I looked at each other before following him. "What can you tell us about the Redline Rogues or the RRs?"

Becker never bothered to get us something to drink, but instead, he took a seat in the living room. We stood.

"I'll repeat what I told the two detectives outside. I have no idea what you're talking about."

"Isn't it true you worked with Marian Ward, Dennis Walters, and Rick Tanner at GM during the eighties?"

"That's true. But I worked with a lot of people. It's common for auto execs to move around between the big three."

"You realize all three of them are dead. They were murdered."

Becker looked down, then back up, but avoided eye contact. "Yes, of course. I'm very saddened by the news. I didn't spend much time with them after I left GM, but I still considered them friends."

"Mr. Becker, we have reason to believe whoever killed them might try to harm you."

"Why?" he asked, his posture stiffening. "I've done nothing."

"That's what we're trying to figure out. We know you were a member of the RRs. Who else knew? *Think*, Mr. Becker. Who might have grievances against you or them?"

Becker ran his hands through what little hair he had. "Look, you guys are sounding like a broken record. I've already answered these questions."

"Then it should be easier the second time around. What are you afraid of? We can protect you."

Becker threw his head back and laughed. "Like how you protected the others?"

The mouth on this guy. Solis was right; he was definitely the short name for Richard.

"Look, I don't need your help."

"Funny, last time I checked, your name was Archie Becker, not Chuck Norris."

Becker shot me a look that rivaled a snotty teenager's. "If you'll excuse me, I have work I need to do."

We may have left his house, but we weren't about to let him leave our sight. I tapped on Solis' window. "This guy's got an attitude and a death wish."

"Told you."

"I want you guys to start interviewing all of the top execs. Start at GM. Maybe we can flush out the other two that way."

We cut the detectives and the patrol car loose and did a drive around the block before parking farther down the street. With only three of the RRs alive, I wanted to make sure it stayed that way.

39

It had been a while since I'd taken on babysitting duty. I had forgotten how slow the hours could drag. Thankfully, Wilkinson could hold a conversation. I remembered being in a similar situation with someone who didn't speak much, and it was painful.

A patrol car had relieved us about an hour earlier and took their position in front of Becker's place. We were four houses down the road, but we were so enjoying our conversation that we stayed put.

Wilkinson and I had chatted all night about everything and anything. I remember there being a lot of silly laughing, and then suddenly his lips were on mine. I don't recall the time or what sparked it, but I didn't pull away. I kissed him back. He had very tender lips that caressed me just so, and he was mindful about not shoving his tongue down my throat right away, either. He worked his way up to it—earned it. When he ran his hand along my cheek and into my hair, I canceled my rule against dating coworkers. It was stupid.

We were like two kids on a date making out in his parents' car. The windows fogged in no time, affording us the privacy we wanted. Soon after, Wilkinson's hand found my breasts. I don't know why, but I tried to play it cool. I didn't want him to know I was already a pile of mush, and as far as my body was concerned, my heavy breaths meant, *don't stop. Hurry. Do everything. I want it all.*

My body was an open house, each part waiting for its inspection. I was in desperate need of a good ravishing. When his fingers caressed my belly button, I remember letting out a premature moan. *Who lets out a moan over a belly button touch?* Anyway, it made my body shiver. I felt safe in his arms and wanted him even more.

He unbuttoned my blouse, and I went to work on his shirt. Undressing in the car wasn't easy. It's nothing like the movies, but it was worth it. It didn't help that we were in a MINI. Thankfully, we had the larger four-door model, and I was tiny. *Hooray for short people.* Wilkinson lowered the parking brake and shoved the stick shift into gear in order to climb over to my side. In one move, he had my seat fully reclined and pushed all the way back. Wilkinson lay against me. His naked pecs pressed against my perky breasts. I didn't mind chest bumping with my partner. Hopefully he would high-five my butt. I pushed his head down and introduced his warm mouth to my tatas. *Lick it. Lick it good.*

I was fully aware of what I was doing. I had given in to Wilkinson. He could do with me whatever he wished. We had crossed the line, and I loved the naughtiness of it.

It didn't take long before the rest of our clothing lay strewn around us. Wilkinson sprung out of his pants against my thigh. I couldn't see the animal, but I swear it felt like another hand having its way with me. He wasn't the only excited one. Moist didn't even come close to capturing what was happening between my legs.

Once again, I thanked the height gods for my shortness; it would have been weird to thank my mother right then. There's no way two normal-sized adults could do what we were doing. He had both my legs pinned back so they rested on his shoulders. I didn't know I had the athleticism in me to become a pretzel. I liked it. I felt exposed, with Wilkinson in complete control. I couldn't stop him from penetrating me—not that I wanted to. From that point on, we were like that bumper sticker. *If this car's a rockin'....*

• • •

The next morning, we were running late for our meeting with White, so we didn't have time to address what had happened the night before. It didn't feel awkward, though. We were both in good moods.

As soon as we entered White's office, I brought him up to speed on what we'd learned from Hardin, and what had happened to him.

"So your real lead came from your conversation with this reporter, not any of the old cases?"

Why is he making this an old case versus new case thing? "Yes. That is, until he was found shot to death. He fed us the names of four RRs. Three of them are dead and we can't get the other to talk, but we've got eyes on him. We plan to follow up on another lead from Hardin: Eddie Bass' daughter."

White conveyed his disapproval with a head shake and a tongue cluck.

"Look, Lieutenant, if Eddie talked to his sister about the RRs, he might have said something to his daughter."

White leaned forward and rested his elbows on his desk. "Let's not get caught up in what happened in the past. Watch Becker, and our killer will eventually show himself—if what you said is true."

"There are two other potential victims. They need to be warned."

White gave us a halfhearted shrug. "It's been on the news. I'm sure they're aware of the situation. Sit on Becker. When our guy makes a move, we'll grab him. Don't go around looking into things you don't need to. You're not here for that, Agent Kane. Is that clear?"

My left eyebrow started to twitch. *He's not the enemy. He's just trying to retire with a pension.* I tempered my emotions as best I could. "With all due respect, Lieutenant White, I don't work for the Detroit Metro Police. I'm a federal agent. I'll investigate this case as I see fit." I should have bitten my tongue, but I was tired of being told what I could and couldn't do on this case. I was FBI. As far as I was concerned, I outranked every uniform there.

I stood. "I will catch this killer. And if there's been a cover-up, I will get to the bottom it. You can be sure of that." I spun around and exited White's office without giving him an opportunity to respond. I didn't care either. I had wasted enough time on this case. *Abby Kane is going rogue.*

Wilkinson caught up with me a few steps outside of White's office.

"You want to tell me what you're doing?"

"We both know we're here to catch the original killer. They never caught him. Garrison took the fall. Who knew how high the corruption in that town went?"

"We can't go it alone."

I stopped and faced him. "We can and we are. I can't trust what we're being told anymore." I continued walking past our office. "You got the car keys?"

"Yeah."

"Good. We're going to Flint."

40

White sat quietly in the back of the dimly lit bar. He held a glass of whiskey with both hands and watched the liquid swirl around. He didn't know what to make of the meeting he'd had with Agent Kane earlier in the morning. She was out of control, and there was nothing he could do. He tried, but it was out of his hands.

But that wasn't good enough for Stevie Roscoe.

"Run me through it one more time," Stevie said.

"I've already told you everything that happened this morning."

"I don't give a fuck," he singsonged slowly. "Do you understand?"

Once more, White went over all the details of his meeting with Kane and Wilkinson.

"She knows there's been a cover-up—that we never got the original guy."

"Does she have proof?"

"Not yet, but she ain't stupid. She's going to figure it out."

Stevie put a finger in White's face. "That bitch ain't figuring out shit."

"I didn't tell her anything," White spat out. "I swear."

Stevie relaxed and returned his hand to his side. He flashed the old cop his trademark smile. "Nobody said you did."

White wasn't buying it, though. Stevie was black rot and he didn't trust him. "I just want to go on record; I did everything asked of me."

Stevie placed a hand on White's glass, stopping it from moving. "Then why the fuck does she think there's a cover-up?"

White looked up from his glass and caught the glare of Stevie's yellow-tinged, green eyes. It was like staring at the devil. White tried to avoid it whenever he could. It was impossible that day. Stevie liked having meetings in tight enclosures, never out in the open. He wanted the person to feel trapped, like there was no way out.

There wasn't.

41

Flint was a little over an hour's drive from downtown Detroit. Traffic was light, so we reached the city limits ten minutes faster. The GPS unit started yapping again when we neared the exit off the highway. Another ten minutes of maneuvering through the city and we found ourselves in a neighborhood where everyone's front yard looked like a public dumping ground. Cars and kitchen appliances were the most popular for lawn decorations.

The small white house on Campbell Road had two cars in its front yard. Neither of them had tires or windows. The house had a tiny, screened-in front porch, overtaken by dead, potted plants and old electronics. I could hear the television before we made it to the porch steps. It sounded like a court case show.

Wilkinson had to knock twice before someone came to the door.

A white lady shoehorned into denim shorts and wearing layered tank tops opened the door. A cigarette hung from her mouth. "Yeah?" she said, adjusting her shirt.

"I'm Agent Kane. This is Agent Wilkinson. We're with the FBI. May we ask you a few questions?"

She looked at us as if she had a choice, like there were options to consider. Eventually, she turned around and walked away, leaving the door open.

I entered the house first. I wished I hadn't. The smell of cat urine nearly destroyed my nose. I didn't bother to hide my reaction either. Wilkinson had a bit more self-control. By my count, there were eight furry felines either walking or lying on the furniture. Our host had already taken her seat in front of the television.

"Are you Lisa Bass?" I asked. She didn't respond, so I picked up the remote and shut the television off.

"Hey, I was watching that."

The strong stench of urine had fouled my mood and left me with little patience. I tried once again, with a little bitch sprinkled in the tone. "Are *you* Lisa Bass?"

"Hell, no," she said, yanking her head back. I could count the chins.

"We were told she might be living here."

"She ain't lived here for over fifteen years. We used to be friends, but we haven't talked since she moved. Why you looking for her?"

"Do you know where she is Ms....?"

"You can call me Michelle, and no, I don't know where she is. Shit, I ain't seen Lisa since she left."

A black and white cat swirled its body around my leg. I could feel the feline's affection vibrating against my calf, but still the animal repulsed me.

Wilkinson spoke up. "It's important we speak with her, Michelle. Any information you have about her whereabouts would be appreciated."

She picked up a cat and scratched it behind the ears. "Well, when she left, she said she was going to school."

"What school?"

Michelle looked at me. "Why do you guys need to talk to her? Is she in trouble?"

"No, she's not. But we believe she has information that can help us with an investigation," I said in a soothing tone, topped off with a smile. I realized nice might be the way to go with Michelle if we wanted any more information. *Suck it up, Abby.*

"Well, she mentioned Oakland, but I don't know if she finished."

We still didn't have a positive ID on Lisa. Claire Bass came up empty. I hoped Michelle wouldn't. "Do you have a picture of Lisa?"

"I might. It'll take some time for me to find it, though, if I do."

I looked around the living room. Michelle was well on her way to being a candidate for the show *Hoarders*. I believed her when she said it might take some time.

"By the way, that ain't her name no more. She changed it to Katherine."

"Katherine Bass?"

"No. Katherine Carter."

42

With a little more prodding and some smiling, I pried Katherine's address from Michelle. Turns out the two talked, but not often. Michelle admitted they had grown apart over the years.

Katherine now lived in a small neighborhood near downtown Detroit. The welcome sign read, "Corktown, Detroit's Oldest Neighborhood, 1834."

"Hmm, I think this is the place Detective Solis was talking about that night," Wilkinson said.

"Impressive," I said as I looked around. The homes might have been built in the early 1800s, but they all looked renovated to their proper glory.

When we pulled up to the two-story, Federal style home with a Range Rover in front of the garage, I understood why Michelle and Katherine had lost touch. Her friend had moved into a higher financial bracket.

I rang the doorbell. We didn't hear dogs yapping, nor did the smell of urine permeate the air. The front steps were peaceful and quiet. A second later, the door opened, and a beautiful woman stood pleasantly in front of us. She wore a white blouse, tucked neatly inside a knee-length black skirt with matching heels. Her hair shined, and her makeup appeared fresh.

"Katherine Carter?"

"Yes, that's me."

I held up my identification. "I'm Agent Abby Kane. This is Agent Trey Wilkinson. May we ask you a few questions?"

"Is something wrong?"

"We're investigating a case and thought you might have information that could help us."

We waited in the sitting room while Katherine went to the kitchen for some bottled water. The décor was vintage yet modern, with lots of warm neutral tones. *I wonder if she hired a designer or watches HGTV.* Pictures lined the mantel above the fireplace. I walked over for a closer look. Most of the pictures were of two little boys, but some included her. *Where was the husband?* Katherine had a ring on—a nice one, too, I might add. *Mental note: schedule a family portrait.*

I was still at the mantel when Katherine paraded back in with her back straight and her long slender neck holding her head at the perfect angle. "Are these your boys?" I asked.

She gently placed the bottles of water on ceramic coasters. "Yes, Lorenzo is eight, and Jackson is four. I've been trying for years to include my husband in our annual picture taking, but I haven't succeeded yet."

"You have beautiful children. My two are similar in age. Ryan is eight and Lucy is five."

Katherine smiled and walked back to the sitting area without saying anything about my children. *Isn't that parent etiquette?* I suddenly didn't feel like drinking her water.

I then watched her sit across from Wilkinson. She crossed her legs, allowing her skirt to ride up high enough to catch Wilky's eye. I immediately cleared my throat. "Are you Lisa Bass, daughter of Eddie Bass of Flint, Michigan?"

Katherine didn't answer us right away. "I'm sorry. It's been awhile since I've heard that name. I've always liked the name Katherine, and—"

"Katherine, we're not here to question you about your name change," Wilkinson said. "We want to talk to you about your father, Eddie."

"My father?"

"Did he ever mention the Redline Rogues or RRs to you?" I asked.

Katherine stared off into the distance before shaking her head. "No, I can't say that I heard him speak about that. Is it the name of a company?"

"The RRs were a group of young executives employed by GM back in the eighties. They were very influential at the time. Some believe they were responsible for having the plant shut down."

"What does that have to do with my father?" she asked, crinkling her nose. "He worked at the factory, on the line."

"A lot of people knew your father. He was a well-liked person—always talking, especially about GM. So much, people called him The Motor."

A smile appeared on Katherine's face. "Yes, he loved the company, until…"

"Until the plant he worked at shut down."

Katherine nodded slowly.

"With your father knowing so much about the company, we thought he might have heard about the RRs and maybe mentioned them to you."

Katherine placed her bottle on a coaster. "If he did, why would he tell me about them? I was just a little girl."

"They were responsible for shutting the plant down in Flint. It's a big topic for conversation."

"That plant was the livelihood of that city. Shutting it down ruined the lives of many families in Flint."

"Including yours?"

Katherine shot me a look. "It killed my father."

The tension in the room had suddenly gone up a notch. "I'm sorry. It must have been tough."

"It was. I still don't know what this has to do with my father."

"We believe someone is killing the RRs. Three of them are already dead. We're trying to locate the rest before it's too late. Claire Bass told us he mentioned the RRs to her. We were hoping he said something to you."

"Claire Bass is a liar. She only encouraged my father by continually talking about the plant; it made him angrier. He drank more because of it."

Katherine had become visibly upset. I figured our chances of getting more information from her were quickly becoming a long shot.

"I have nothing else to say. Now if you don't mind, I'm busy." She stood and held her arm out to the door.

We thanked her for her time, and I handed her my card. "If you think of anything, call me."

43

Katherine peeked from behind the window curtain as the two agents returned to their hideous yellow car.

Preston Carter also kept an eye on the two visitors as well, except he watched from a basement window. Behind him, a naked young woman lay on a wooden table. Her arms and legs were held in place by straps attached at each corner. Duct tape covered her mouth, and tears ran down her face.

Preston put his scalpel down on a counter and removed the clear plastic apron he wore. "I'll be back, my darling." He kissed the woman's forehead before heading upstairs.

"Katherine!" he called as he burst into the hallway.

She appeared from the kitchen. "What is it, dear?"

"Who were those two people? What did they want?"

Katherine could see that her husband was flustered and becoming increasingly agitated. She cleared a few strands from his left eye. "There's nothing to worry about, dear. They wanted to talk to me about my father."

"They're the police, aren't they? They're on to us. I knew it. We should have taken a break. There wasn't enough time between kills—"

A large cracking noise emanated from Katherine's open hand as it slammed into Preston's face, sending his head off to the side. It was the only thing that worked when he slipped into a panic.

Preston held his left cheek, his head still turned to the side, looking down.

"I told you not to worry. You must trust me, darling. I have a plan. You do want to help me with my plan, don't you?"

Preston nodded slowly. He did want to help his beautiful wife—anything for his queen.

He had first noticed Katherine in his freshman biology class. He was a tenured professor and she was a first year student, twenty at the time. The day she first entered his lab, her hair was pulled loosely back into a ponytail, and she had a horrendous orange backpack slung over her shoulders, but she looked as if angels were carrying her in. Her sweet smile was infectious. Her eyes could calm the most cantankerous of people. Preston watched her search for a seat, but didn't stop there. He continued to sneak peeks throughout the entire class period. By all accounts, she was the most beautiful woman he had ever laid eyes upon.

During the second quarter of her first year, Preston noticed a difference in Katherine. In ways, she was a lot like him. She had tendencies, as he liked to describe it. She once took a lab frog and sliced it horizontally from head to toe— a total of two hundred eighty-five slices. Preston knew, because he counted each one. She did the same with a frozen dog using a surgical saw. He continued to push her young mind. After a year and a half, he felt she was ready. He gave her a body. She didn't ask who it had been or where it had come from. She didn't care. She went right to work.

When the two started to date, that had been the turning point, and Katherine accompanied Preston on a kill. It was the start of a wonderful partnership. The Doctor had taken on an apprentice. For the next two years, Katherine learned from him. So much so that she started advising him on how to continue forward with his hobby without getting caught. Preston had hoped they could become a duo, but Katherine was much more comfortable with the planning. Though she *had* developed an affinity for scalping people.

"I'm worried," Preston finally mumbled.

"Don't be, sweetie. I haven't failed us yet, and I don't intend to." Katherine slipped her hand down the front of his pants and fondled him. Preston shut his eyes and let out a breathy growl. "Now go back downstairs and finish up with your play date. When you're done, you can tell me all about it."

44

Later that afternoon, we met Solis and Madero at a Coney Island restaurant in Birmingham. They had spent most of the week interviewing executives at GM and Ford and making sure Archie Becker didn't end up dead.

Both detectives were eating chili dogs when we arrived. I looked at Wilkinson; his eyes lit up like a dog eyeing a large soup bone. He had become addicted to chili dogs. *What is it with guys and chili?*

"Agents," Solis said. "Please, have a seat."

We sat opposite them in the booth and placed our orders immediately. As soon as the waitress left, Solis wasted no time brushing off his hands and updating us.

"We interviewed every top-level executive at GM. Either there are no other RRs working there or someone is holding back. Same with Ford. We're heading over to Chrysler tomorrow."

Not what I wanted to hear. "How's our guy doing?"

"Nothing's changed. He goes to work and comes home. We tried talking to him again, but he insists he doesn't know what we're talking about."

"He's got interesting nighttime habits though," Madero added. "We took over the night shift and discovered our guy sneaks out near midnight and spends time at Belle Isle."

"How long has this been going on?"

Solis shrugged. "He's done it twice on our watch. We park down the street so he thinks no one is watching."

"What's down at Belle Isle?" Wilkinson asked.

"It's a popular late-night hangout for young people, like a make-out area, except our guy hangs out where there aren't any women."

"Why are you letting him leave the house?" I asked.

"Look, Agent Kane, we can't stop him. He's a free man."

"Yeah, well, we're tagging along tonight." If Becker insisted on endangering his life like this, I didn't want to rely on these two to keep him safe.

45

Solis radioed us around midnight. Wilkinson and I were parked five houses down from the Becker residence. Solis and Madero were at the opposite end of the street, two houses away, so they still had eyes on his front door.

"Our guy is on the move," he said. "He's in a black Ford Explorer and should be passing you any second."

"All right. Hang back and let us pick him up," I answered.

Wilkinson waited until the Explorer rounded the corner before pulling onto the road, fearful Becker might recognize the Yellow Jacket. It wasn't the best vehicle for surveillance.

The traffic was light on the highway, so we kept our distance, maybe a hundred yards or so behind. Solis and Madero tailed us. We weren't worried about losing Becker. We knew his destination. Thirty minutes later, we crossed MacArthur Bridge.

Belle Isle was literally a nine-hundred-acre island park in the middle of the Detroit River. During the day, people picnicked and swam, visited the zoo and the botanical gardens, and just enjoyed the outdoors. However, at night, the action took place inside their vehicles.

We kept our distance from Becker, blending with the other late-night visitors cruising the scene. There seemed to be a lot of young people hanging in and outside of their cars, mostly college students from the look of it. Farther down the road, though, I could see that the area got desolate.

Becker drove at a parade's pace. I was not sure what he was looking at; women didn't seem to do it for him. Maybe he liked young men.

"It might be a good idea to follow by foot," I said. "The crowd's thinning and he might pick up on us."

"Good idea."

We parked near the end of the crowd. I radioed Solis and Madero that we had feet on the ground and told them to sit back for a bit.

I moved swiftly along the trees. I didn't bother to look back; I could hear Wilkinson in step behind me. There was little chance Becker could see us where we were. Unfortunately, the dark afforded Becker the same advantage. He had parked under a large tree, making it nearly impossible to see inside his vehicle. It didn't help that scattered clouds prevented most of the moonlight from reaching the ground.

We moved in as close as we could, maybe fifty yards away, and watched. Fifteen minutes passed before a slow-moving vehicle pulled into the stall next to Becker. A man exited and quickly entered the passenger side of Becker's Explorer.

"Did you get a good look at him?" Wilkinson asked.

"Not really, but I have a pretty good idea of what's about to go down." I looked around for a closer vantage point. Becker's safety concerned me more than his sexual escapades. For all we knew, that stranger could be the killer.

"I don't feel comfortable sitting back. I'm going to move up to that tiny bush near the car."

"It's out in the open. They'll see you."

Advantage #23 for someone with my height: I can squat at night and look like a bush. "Don't worry; I'll blend. If I still can't see what's going on, I'll radio you and we'll break up Becker's party." I gave Solis and Madero the heads up on the plan.

"I'll be right here," Wilkinson said as he sent me on my way with a pat to the butt.

I made my way around a few trees and a couple of tall shrubs. I lost sight of the car for a few seconds, but I picked up a visual soon enough. I crouched, waited a beat, and then scurried to the tiny bush near the car. I was now one with the shrub.

From my low angle looking up into the vehicle, I had an unobstructed view. A faint glow, probably from the entertainment system, lit them up enough to know what they were doing. It was make-out city all right.

• • •

Wilkinson stayed put and watched the car. He had lost sight of Abby until she reappeared, running to the bush. She did indeed blend in. From what he could see, it looked like she had an eyeline into the vehicle. The agent raised his radio, ready to ask her for an update, when a twig snapped behind him. He spun around and reached for his weapon at the same time. That's when he saw her.

"Agent Wilkinson, it's me, Katherine Carter."

Katherine, Wilkinson thought. *What is she doing here?* He relaxed a little and took his hand off his weapon. "Mrs. Carter, why are you here?" The situation was confusing, but from the way she had her arms wrapped around herself, she appeared to be either cold or frightened.

"I'm so glad I found you," she said, approaching him and letting her arms fall to the side. Before he could answer, she swung her right arm up and across his neckline.

It took a moment for Wilkinson to comprehend what had happened. He reached up and felt the warm liquid pouring from his neck. *No! It can't be. Not you!*

Katherine backed away, out of his reach. Dappled moonlight crossed her face revealing a smile. He tried to speak but could only manage a gurgle. Wilkinson knew he had to act fast if he wanted any chance of survival. He also had to warn Abby.

46

Becker had had enough fun. I didn't want to bust up the party when they were rounding third base, let alone home plate. I radioed Wilkinson to move in, but he didn't answer. Again I hit the talk button on the two-way. "Wilkinson, I'm moving in. Respond." Still nothing. I knew he had eyes on me, so I figured I'd go ahead and he would see me.

The radio crackled. "What's going on?" Solis asked.

"I can't get a hold of Wilkinson. I need you guys to move in. I'm proceeding toward the vehicle."

Just as I stood up, my eyes caught movement near the trees. Wilkinson had made his way into the open. His body movement wasn't right. He looked drunk. His arms weren't swinging either. I watched for a moment before I headed towards him. As I got closer, it became clearer; he had both hands around his neck.

"What's wrong?" I asked picking up the pace. "Wilky!"

He didn't answer. When I reached him, I understood why. The blood was everywhere. He fell to his knees. So did I. His bloody hands were gripped tightly around his neck, but they slipped for a second, and a red arc shot pass my face until he could reclaim his grip. I placed my hands over his, helping to keep pressure.

"What happened? Who did this?" I asked.

He opened his mouth and moved it but nothing came out. His eyes were wide and locked onto me. He was scared.

"Hold on Wilky. We're going to get through this."

I grabbed my radio. "Solis, Wilkinson's down. I need an ambulance. Wilkinson is *down*. Get an ambulance here *now*!" I dropped the radio and put my other hand back over his. "You're going to be fine. I've got a grip on you."

I could hear his labored breathing, wet with his blood loss. It worried me. He was fading fast. His eyes blinked rapidly and then closed. I slapped his face. "Stay with me, Wilky. I need you to stay awake." *If not for yourself, do it for me.*

His eyes opened, but he might as well have been staring right through me. *This can't be happening.*

The sound of a door opening grabbed my attention. I looked up in enough time to see the tall man exit Becker's vehicle and get into his. Within seconds, he had the Mercedes backing up. I could hear the gears in the car shifting. The wheels squealed as the car sped off. I couldn't leave Wilkinson.

"Stop," I shouted, "FBI." Any hope in stopping our guy faded fast as I watched the rear lights of the vehicle get smaller.

A car screeched to a halt near us.

"What the fuck happened?" Solis shouted, exiting the vehicle.

"Wilkinson is bleeding from the neck, badly. Someone attacked him after we separated."

"Becker," I motioned with my head, "check on him."

Solis ran over to the car while Madero grabbed a medical kit from their trunk.

I dug through the kit with one hand while I gave orders to Madero. "The bridge. There's only one way off the island. Our guy is in a silver SUV."

Madero jumped back into the unmarked car and sped off in the opposite direction, hoping to reach the bridge before the Mercedes did.

I put a big piece of gauze over Wilky's wound. It seemed to help. It's what I wanted to believe. I looked at his eyes; he no longer had the deer stuck in the headlights look. It took all I could to hide my emotions. I needed to remain strong and let him know we would get through this. "Hang in there, Wilky; help is on the way."

"Fuck!" Solis shouted.

That's not what I wanted to hear. I looked back over my shoulder.

"Becker's dead. He's fucking dead!"

I couldn't believe it. It all had happened so quickly. Had I lost complete control of everything?

47

Earlier, when Preston had entered the Explorer, Archie Becker had already had a playful smile on his face. "I've missed you," he said. "You don't return my calls."

Preston leaned in, and they kissed for a while before he pulled away. "I'm sorry. I've been busy. It's exam time, you know."

"Always the teacher."

"A mind is a terrible thing to waste. Isn't that the phrase?"

"What about a hard-on?" Becker batted his eyelashes as he reached over and grabbed Preston by his crotch. "Looks like teacher is hot for student." He stroked the professor through his trousers while they kissed noisily.

"That's nice," Preston mumbled. He then unzipped his pants and freed himself for Becker, who stroked him for a bit longer before lowering his head and sucking greedily. The professor closed his eyes and leaned back as he imagined his beautiful wife Katherine in his lap, lizard licking his head before swallowing him whole. Preston wasn't into guys, but he was into killing them. Whatever it took. That's what he did. Plus, Becker gave surprisingly decent head.

• • •

Katherine had known the police were watching Becker's home—a minor inconvenience and nothing to be concerned about. They would have to lock him up if they wanted to keep him safe. And even then, she vowed she would find a way to get to him. Nothing would deter her from the plan—not even a couple of federal agents. She still had the upper hand.

It didn't take much for her to convince her husband to spend time with Becker. He had an insatiable appetite he needed to fill. Because of that, he would be capable of letting another man suck him off. A mouth was a mouth, she told him.

Preston had earlier meetings with Becker, all of them trial runs. The engineer was a nervous nelly, and Katherine felt the need to practice to get it right. She always followed her husband in a separate car on each occasion and parked on the other side of the park. She then kept watch on Preston from the bushes. The trial runs had rid her plan of any kinks, and the time had come for Becker to learn what it would be like to watch the life spray out of him.

When the agents appeared, it didn't surprise Katherine. She had prepared for their meddling ways. *Look at the big bad agents, kneeling exactly where I thought they would.* Becker always parked in the same stall. He liked to think the big oak tree hid his nasty habit.

Like clockwork, the pawns in her plan had assumed their positions. When Katherine saw the small one break away, she didn't think things could get any better. *Never leave your partner. Isn't that FBI 101?* She sent Preston a text, "They're here. Do it now."

Too bad the tall one remained behind, she thought as she made her way toward him. *I so wanted the little one.*

48

Wilkinson hung on until help arrived, but he didn't do well on the ride to the hospital. I was with him inside the ambulance when he died. He had lost so much blood; the EMT couldn't do much. I asked if I could be alone with him, and the medic moved up to the front seat with the driver.

Only then did I allow myself to cry. I didn't think I could wait until I got back to my hotel. I did my best to keep quiet as I choked back most of my tears. I brushed a few strands of hair away from his eyes. *You always watched out for me. Where was I when you needed someone watching over you?* The EMT had bandaged his throat and covered him up to his neck in sheets. All I had to look at was his face. That's all I wanted anyway.

Oh, Wilky. I wanted to think it was a terrible dream, that I would wake up the next morning and have another day with him, with the two of us fighting over directions for the fastest route just so we could keep talking to each other when it got quiet. I wanted to see him fidget with his Oakland A's ball cap and flash his warm smile. I hadn't had enough of playing cat and mouse with our feelings for each other, as though we had all the time in the world.

All those "wish" thoughts started to flood my head—things I wished I had said or done with him. *Why is it we never take full advantage of those we have around us?* I remembered having these exact same feelings with Peng. Even though I had done so much more with Peng than with any man before, I could have given more of myself. I wish I had.

Wilky and I had grown closer than ever on this case. That night in the car turned the corner for us. I wondered if it was better that we hadn't gone further down the road sooner. Would the pain have been more?

I knew I had to pull myself together and disregard the emptiness in my stomach. I wiped my nose on my sleeve and dried my eyes. They felt puffy—not the look a head investigator wants to show.

I stuck around the hospital for a bit, but there really wasn't much I could do there. I got into a cab and headed back to Belle Isle, where I knew I could be useful.

I cried the entire ride.

Solis and Madero were still at the scene, along with an army of uniforms searching the park and interviewing people. The late-night partiers had abandoned their cars and were pressed up against the police tape, watching people they normally saw on a detective show.

I didn't have to say anything about Wilkinson's death; word had already spread.

"I'm sorry," Solis said. "I hate to see any member of law enforcement fall."

"He was a good guy," Madero added.

I appreciated their words, even Madero's. But as hard as it was, I had to put Wilkinson's death behind me—not because I didn't care, but because I needed to focus.

I remembered spending a year searching for the degenerates who took Peng's life. I worked late nights, gave up weekends and holidays, but I never found out who did it. That became my first and only unsolved case. I swore on the ride back from the hospital that I would catch Wilkinson's killer.

I filled in Solis and Madero on everything that had happened, from the moment Wilkinson and I left our car, to when we parted ways, to when they arrived and my partner was down.

"There are two killers," Solis said.

"There has to be," I said. "Both Wilkinson and Archie Becker received similar wounds to their necks at roughly the same time."

"You sure Becker was alive before Wilkinson showed up?" Solis asked.

"Positive. I saw his face before his head started to bob up and down in the other guy's lap."

Solis pointed to the tree line. "That's when Wilkinson came stumbling out from the shadows."

"Correct. In the amount of time it took me to make my way over to Wilkinson, Becker had to have been killed by the blond guy that sped off. You need a team to pull that off."

49

My supervisor, Special Agent Reilly, urged me to stay in Detroit instead of coming back for Wilkinson's funeral.

"Absolutely not," I said. "It's only two days. I'll be back in Detroit before you know it."

Reilly was in a sticky spot. On the one hand, he could have ordered me to stay in Detroit. On the other hand, Wilkinson was my partner. Plus, I wanted to see my family. I missed them.

I hopped on an 8:50 a.m. Delta flight that put me in San Francisco around eleven that same morning. I was eager to see everyone. I couldn't have stopped my bouncing knee, even if I'd wanted.

It was Saturday, so I had the weekend with the kids. I called Po Po as soon as I landed to let her know I would be home shortly. Traffic into the city was light. Before I knew it, the cab had made a right onto Pfeiffer Street.

"Mommmmy!" Lucy squealed as I walked into the house. She ran toward me and nearly knocked me over as I kneeled and wrapped my arms around her. Ryan joined us. I grabbed him and hugged and kissed them both. I didn't want to let go. It felt so right. "It's so good to be home."

"Are you finished with work?" Ryan asked.

"I'm sorry, not yet. But let's not think about that. How about we go to the Academy of Sciences today?"

Both kids cheered. They had been bugging me to go to the museum, Ryan especially, for a while now. He wanted to see Claude, the albino alligator.

"Go get ready."

I stood up and hugged Po Po.

"We all miss you," she said. "So sorry about your friend. Does he have a family?"

"His parents and one sister. No family of his own, though."

Po Po shook her head. Thankfully, she turned away and headed into the kitchen. I didn't want to spend time talking about it. I wanted to focus on the family.

We spent the entire day at the Golden Gate Park, where the museum was located. Ryan and Lucy loved the hands-on exhibits. Even Po Po had a good time. After we were done with the museum, we picked a quiet spot in the park where we relaxed and ate sandwiches.

From the shade of a tree, Po Po and I watched Ryan and Lucy play tag with a bunch of other children. I stretched out on the blanket, enjoying the crisp weather. The sun shined above while a slight breeze kept us cool—such a departure from the muggy heat I had to deal with in Detroit. I would pack jeans, light blouses, and tennis shoes for the remainder of my time in Detroit. Screw the suits. They weren't required dress.

"When you coming home for good?" Po Po asked.

"That's a hard question to answer."

"Why?"

I didn't want to get into the details of the case, nor did I want to explain why catching a criminal took so long. I really had no interest in bringing home my work, especially that day.

"It's complicated." Boy was it ever. Up until now, Wilkinson and I had avoided mentioning our suspicions of a cover-up to Reilly. Questions being asked at his level, especially since we had no hard evidence to prove our suspicions, would just make matters worse. As far as he knew, we were progressing on the case.

50

Wilkinson was put to rest in his hometown of Berkeley, across the bay from where I lived. Reilly insisted on driving me, though I had a feeling he really wanted a little Q&A time regarding the report I'd written for Wilkinson's death.

We exchanged five minutes of pleasantries, more than I had anticipated. After that, he got to the point.

"I want you to go over it again," Reilly said.

"Everything I have to say was in the report I gave you."

"I want to hear it. We lost a good agent, and the department isn't exactly thrilled about it."

You think I'm planning a party? We were all affected by Wilkinson's death. We lost a *great* agent and *great* friend. I took a deep breath and once again walked Reilly through that night.

"So you snuck up to the vehicle for a closer look?"

"That's correct," I said.

"Why didn't Wilkinson advance with you?"

"My height. For cover, I used a tiny bush out in the open, not far from the car. I could scrunch down and look like part of it. Wilkinson couldn't. But he had eyes on me the entire time."

Reilly shot me a look of disbelief.

"I'm not kidding. I'm short. He's not."

"So he could see you, but you couldn't see him?"

"That's right."

"Now that we know there are two killers, the case is much more dangerous. I can't have you working alone. I'll send out another agent."

"That won't be necessary," I said, motioning with my hand. "I have it under control."

"Agent Kane, I can't risk anything happening to you. I'm sending out another agent."

"Another agent will only get in the way. There's too much catching up to do. I have two detectives dedicated to these cases at my disposal." *Sure they aren't that bright, but still, they've been there from the start and know what's going on.*

"That doesn't help your case," Reilly said with a shake of his head.

"Give me two weeks on my own. If I haven't put it to bed by then, you can send an army of agents my way."

Reilly didn't say anything, only stared straight ahead at the road. After a few moments of silence, he turned to me. "Two weeks, not a day more."

"Deal!"

"And I want updates twice a week."

Not a problem. I wanted to nail these sickos. Dead or alive, it didn't matter.

51

The Carters decided to spend family day at the zoo. Lorenzo and Jackson led the way straight to the butterfly garden. It was their favorite exhibit and a family tradition to start there. Hundreds of free-flying, colorful wonders flapped around the two boys the second they entered the habitat. The boys' smiles hung open as they twirled, unsure of which of the butterflies to follow.

"Lorenzo, keep an eye on your brother," Katherine called out. She and Preston took a seat on a bench inside the enclosed exhibit, where it was always a balmy seventy-five degrees. It bothered Katherine, mostly because of what it did to her hair.

Preston picked at his fingernails. "I'm worried," he said.

Katherine knew her husband saw the glass as half empty; she needed to inject some positivity into the situation. She turned to him and fixed his collar, then dusted off his sports coat. "We're almost finished. Soon we'll go back in hiding and back to our randoms." That's what she liked to call them.

Preston put on a smile, but Katherine could see the strain in his jaw. She gave his thigh a playful pat and then rubbed it up and down. He turned to her. "We almost got caught. What makes you think they don't know who we are by now?"

"They're too focused on Archie Becker. They don't have a clue who we are, even after that night."

Preston looked into the calm eyes of his wife. "I'd like to keep it that way, but... you killed an FBI agent. Won't that bring more attention?"

"You must trust me, darling. I have no intention of messing up what we have." She flashed her husband her trademark smile and gave his thigh one last squeeze, her way of saying, "Pull it together."

Katherine followed the rollercoaster path of a large blue and yellow butterfly in front of her. "I'll tell you what; we'll watch the agent for a few days and see what she knows, and then we'll consider how we make our next move."

"That sounds much better," Preston said as he stood. "Come on. Let's find the boys. It's feeding time for the lions."

The same butterfly now circled in front of him. Its wingspan was nearly five inches from tip to tip. They both watched it land near the edge of the pathway. Preston stopped to admire the beautiful creature, before stepping down on it and twisting back and forth with his shoe. When he lifted his loafer, all that was left on the pathway was a bluish stain. Katherine simply smiled. The boys weren't the only ones who loved the butterfly exhibit.

52

The Detroit heat was a sticky reminder that I was back on the case. I was the driver, so I said no to renting a yellow MINI and got myself a pair of balls—a three-hundred horsepower Chevy Impala. It painted a nice analogy for where my mind was.

I had two weeks to take these killers down and I wasn't about to waste any time. Sending extra manpower could trigger the worst; the killers could get spooked and head back underground. They did it once; they could do it again. I needed them to think they were safe, that they could keep killing without any repercussions.

I would have to count on Solis and Madero for more help—even White, though I still didn't trust the old guy. They may not be the most effective allies, but I had to make it work. Those were the cards I'd accepted. I had to play them.

That night at Belle Isle, Madero fell short on cutting off the SUV, but I had gotten a partial on the license plate—a long shot, but I hoped something would pop up. We also had a description on one of our killers. He was male, had blond hair, stood roughly six feet tall and looked to be in shape. It sounded like any generic male, but a lead was a lead.

Still, the kink in our investigation was discovering there were two of them. No one suspected a killing team. Nothing in the previous investigation or murders indicated there were two people involved. If they were a team now, were they a team seven years ago? I wished I knew the answer to that question.

I had my personal take on what went down at Belle Isle. While we were busy watching the car, one of them watched us. I only had one question regarding that scenario: how did the other killer get the jump on Wilkinson?

I finally arrived at my hotel at four in the afternoon. I had plans to unload my luggage and then head over to central precinct, but Solis called.

"Agent Kane, we found her."

"Who?"

"The fifth RR."

53

Katherine Carter sat quietly in her Rover in the parking lot of Daimler Chrysler. She had been keeping tabs on Ellen Scott for a few weeks now and was busy making final preparations to set Preston loose on her as early as that night. Those plans went out the window when she saw the executive being escorted out of the building by the two detectives. She watched Ellen and one of them get into her car. They then followed another car out of the parking structure. Katherine reached for her cell and hit speaker.

"Preston, dear, there's a change of plans."

"What? Why? I was so looking forward to it. Must we?"

"We must. It's unfortunate, but the two detectives showed up at Ellen's work, and they have just left with her. Now, I don't want you to worry, but do you remember our emergency plans?"

"Why are you asking me? Do they know it's us?"

"No, dear, but we must be prepared. I'm assuming they're going to question her. Remember our plans, and everything will work itself out. I'll call you later."

Katherine followed Ellen and the detectives. At first. she thought they would whisk the executive away into protective custody, but when they pulled into a Coney Island, she realized there was no urgency. Once again, Katherine was in the mindset that Ellen's time on Earth would be coming to an end.

She waited patiently outside the Coney Island while she visualized scenarios of what could go wrong. None of it bothered her, of course. She had a plan in place should the police question Ellen at her office and discover something. She also had a plan in place should the police put Ellen into protective custody. Heck, she even had a plan if they decided to question her at a random location, like the one they were at.

Katherine smiled and mentally patted herself on the back. *Such stupid people.*

Her evil smile turned when the petite agent showed up. From the moment Kane had appeared on Katherine's doorstep, wanting to question her, she disliked the woman. She couldn't stand the way she looked: tiny, bouncy, and pretending to be tough. *Ugh.* It annoyed Katherine. It didn't help that she couldn't stand the way the agent walked, talked, laughed, and flipped her hair back; she obviously had a crush on her partner. *That's come to an end, hasn't it? Ha!*

Anybody could have seen right through the agent's pathetic defenses that day at the house. The way she looked at what's-his-name, Katherine half expected Kane to start drooling uncontrollably. Even when they left, she walked closer to him than normal for people who worked together. Katherine didn't blame Kane. She herself wouldn't mind sharing a bed with the hunky agent. And while she did kill him, the only pleasure she received from it was knowing it would hurt the tough little crime fighter.

She watched Kane cross the parking lot and enter the restaurant. *I have a plan for you. I just thought of it. It's very simple. Kill you last.*

54

I walked by the row of red, vinyl booths until I reached the one Solis and Madero had squeezed into. A female executive dressed in an ash-gray skirt suit sat across from them. She had her red hair pulled back off of her pale face, giving me a clear look at her narrowing eyes and pursed lips. Not the reaction I was expecting. I pulled up a chair and sat in front of the booth.

"Solis. Madero." I nodded.

Solis made the introduction. "This is Agent Kane. She's with the FBI and is here to help."

I stuck my hand out. "Pleasure to meet you, Ms…"

She uncrossed her arms. "Ellen Scott, but you may call me Ellen."

Solis started briefing me. "Ms. Scott identified herself as an RR during our interview two hours ago. She's the director of Marketing—"

"Public relations. I head up public relations for the company," she quickly corrected.

"She's also aware that a killer has been targeting auto executives," Solis continued. "Considering what happened to Becker, we thought it was important to get Ms. Scott into a secure location. We're awaiting word on where it will be."

"Agent Kane," Ellen said, "is it true that I'm next?"

"We have reason to believe you are in danger. But you must know, the FBI, along with the Detroit Police Department, will do everything in our power to keep you safe. We're not going to let any harm come to you."

"Really? I think about the others and how you failed to keep them safe and, well…"

What's with the attitude? We're here to help. "Ellen, I know this is a difficult time for you, but I need to ask you a few questions."

"Fine." Ellen went back to crossing her arms across her chest.

"Tell me what you know about the Redline Rogues."

Ellen spoke frankly. "Dennis Walters was the leader, a very dynamic individual at the time. He was on the fast track to the top, and we were all enamored with him. He was the model of how to get ahead. So naturally, I and other like-minded individuals were attracted to him—probably the reason why the group worked so well."

"Dennis started the group and then recruited people?"

"That I'm not clear on," Ellen said as she fidgeted with her nails. "I was the youngest and the last to join. The group had been established for almost a year before they recruited me."

"Why did they stop recruiting after you?"

"Dennis wanted the group kept small so we could stay under the radar and push our agenda. Plus, we were the best."

I'm sure you thought you were. "Tell us about this agenda."

"Get ahead by any means possible. That was the goal."

"Looks like you cracked the big time," Solis said.

Ellen didn't bother looking at either detective, preferring only to address me. "We all got what we wanted."

I turned to Solis. "What about the other RRs?" Before he could answer, Ellen started to speak.

"Detective Solis asked me about that earlier, but as I *told* him, there were only *five* of us, not six."

Hmm. Hardin had been correct with his other information, why did he get this wrong?

"Are you sure?" I asked. "I mean you were the last to join the group. Maybe there were others you didn't know about or even a silent member."

"I highly doubt that," Ellen said, her nose angled slightly up. "We divided the work evenly amongst us all. Plus, we each brought a skill set to the table."

"I understand that, but do you think it could be possible?"

Ellen thought for a moment. "I guess, but I don't understand why that person would be hidden from us."

"Or you," I added. "Tell me about the group's involvement with the plant closings in Flint."

"There's not much to tell. At the time, the company rewarded employees that came up with cost saving initiatives. Dennis wanted to take advantage of it. We spent our weekends brainstorming at his place, sometimes ten to twelve hours a day."

"That's where the idea to shut down plants was born?"

Ellen looked at everyone at the table before speaking. "Yes. Closing plants would save GM millions. It would allow us to move the money saved into projects benefitting us."

"Are you for real?" Solis said. "Did you guys even think about the people who would get the axe, not to mention the public relations nightmare for the company?"

"We did and we didn't. Anyway, we felt if we could get the right support internally, we could pull it off."

"If a plant was underperforming, wouldn't it be a no-brainer to close it?" I asked.

"Yes."

"So what made this a brilliant, cost-saving idea if it was common practice to close a plant that didn't do well?"

Ellen hesitated for a moment and then looked me in the eye. "None of the plants we closed were underperforming. We falsified the information."

55

They lied!

I thought I had heard wrong, but Ellen continued to reaffirm what she said. "So GM closed plants that were doing just fine?"

"Yes."

"What were you guys thinking? Thousands of individuals had their livelihoods ruined because of this decision."

"You don't understand. We were young, hungry… look, we had pressures to succeed."

I looked around the table at the others with my jaw unhinged. I couldn't believe what she was saying. *Pressure? Success?* "You're going to have to come up with a better answer than that."

Ellen jerked back. "Those plants were borderline. They could have made a turn for the worse at any moment. I don't think we were wrong in making this recommendation—"

"Just advantageous."

Ellen turned away, shaking her head.

"Wouldn't the company see that the plants didn't need to be closed?" Solis asked.

"Dennis was a master at numbers. He could bend them to support anything. Everyone had a role to play."

"And what about you?" I inquired. "Were you tasked with keeping people silent? Did you keep Eddie Bass silent?"

Ellen shot me a darting gaze.

"Surprise. Yeah, we know about Eddie Bass," I said.

"Eddie Bass was a liability," Ellen shot back. "His big mouth always got him in trouble. How did you know about us?"

Us? This is new. Keep her going, Abby. "His sister mentioned it. She said Eddie talked about you guys."

"Is he the one behind this, the killings?"

"Eddie's dead, Ellen."

Her posture deflated a bit. "Oh, I hadn't heard."

"I doubt you heard much about what happened to all those workers," Madero added.

For once, I agreed with Madero. The three of us were disgusted with Ellen Scott. What she, the RRs, did for their selfish gains made me sick. And now we were charged with keeping that woman alive. The fact that we didn't like her made it even tougher.

"How did you keep Eddie from mouthing off more than he already had?"

Ellen swallowed as she shifted in her seat. For the first time, she looked uncomfortable. "Sex and money," she said bluntly.

I gave Solis and Madero a look.

"What?" Ellen asked indignantly. "It kept him quiet."

I didn't expect to hear that. He was The Motor. "That's it? Sexual favors and money?"

"More or less."

"How much money are we talking here?"

"Couple thousand. Eddie was a simple man."

"Had the plant already closed when these favors were given?"

Ellen sat there, refusing to say anything else. I tried nicely to get her to talk, but she held her ground. And then she rolled her eyes.

"You're starting to piss me off. You know what happens when you piss off a federal agent?"

Ellen looked away and then examined her nails before looking back at me. "Are you guys here to protect me, or are you here to investigate what happened years ago?" She leaned back and folded her arms, again.

Temper, Abby. Temper. I took a breath and exhaled. "Look, we're trying to help here."

"I've already said enough. Now, if you would excuse me." Ellen motioned for me to move over to the side.

"Where are you going?"

"I've changed my mind about your help. I don't want it. You did a terrible job at keeping Archie Becker safe. I have no reason to believe you can do any better for me. I'll take my chances."

I scooted my chair over, still pleading with Ellen. She ignored me. We watched her storm out of the restaurant and drive away.

56

I didn't care whether Ellen Scott died or not. She was no better than the killers. But the truth was, I needed her alive. So long as she was above ground with that sniveling look on her face, our killers would remain above ground.

Hearing what the Redline Rogues did was despicable. I'm sure all Ellen cared about was covering her butt. She was the only one alive, and if the RRs were investigated, she would likely take the rap for it. *What was better: dying at the hands of a vigilante killer or going to jail?* I would have asked Ellen what she preferred, but her walking out on us gave me my answer.

I had a job to do. If Ellen wanted to make it easier by offering herself up as bitch bait, fine by me.

"Now what?" Solis asked.

"We can't afford to let anything happen to Ellen. If the killers get to her, I'm afraid they'll go underground again. I want a car at her house. I also want the two of you on her."

"Got it." Madero then picked up the menu while Solis motioned for the waitress.

"What are you two doing? When I say I want you guys on her, that means starting now."

"But we haven't eaten yet."

"Look, there are two places Ellen is probably heading to right now: back to work or home. Wherever she ends up, you can call to have a pizza delivered to your location."

Madero rolled his eyes as he put the menu down. I didn't care. He could stand to lose a few. I had two weeks. I couldn't afford to have either one of them dragging their feet.

"When she's settled, let me know and I'll meet up with you guys," I called out as the detectives walked away.

In the meantime I had plans to head back to Belle Isle. Someone watched us that night. I hoped a fresh look at the area would tell me who.

57

"Who does she think she is?" Madero whined. "I'm a grown man. She can't tell me when I can and cannot eat. That's bullshit."

Solis rolled down his window. "The sooner this case gets put to bed, the sooner she'll be out of our business."

"Easy for you to say. She likes you. The bitch never speaks to me."

"Maybe it's because you're condescending to her."

"Fuck that. I'm condescending to everyone. Hey, our girl just made a left. Looks like she's heading home." Madero then made a hard right into a Taco Bell drive thru.

Solis grabbed hold of the armrest to steady himself. "What are you doing?"

"Getting some of my people's food."

"Taco Bell is your people's food?"

"Close enough. We'll be in and out. Plus, you got the address."

What Madero said was true. Taco Bell had reasonably good drive thru times. Unfortunately, the lady in front appeared to be making her very first trip to a fast food restaurant, and the menu board proved to be overwhelming.

After what seemed like a half hour, Madero leaned into the horn. "Come on lady. It's the same fucking ingredients, just rearranged differently. Shit, man."

"I always wondered about that. The only difference between a tostada and a taco is a tostada is flat. Why the two?"

"It's easier to eat a taco," Madero said.

"So why keep the tostada if it's just a flat hard-to-eat taco?"

"Hey, the Italians do the same thing. What's the difference between a straight noodle and a curly noodle? They taste the same, but they pretend like they got different dishes."

"It's the sauce that makes it different."

"Every sauce is made from tomatoes."

"No, they're not."

Madero finally reached the menu and focused his attention there. He turned to Solis. "You know what you want?"

"Yeah. One beef burrito supreme, two steak taco supremes, and a large Coke."

Madero turned back to the menu board. "Okay, give me two beef burrito supremes, one seven layer burrito, four steak taco supremes, one gordita, an order of nachos, some cinnamon twists, and a meximelt. Oh, and two large Cokes."

"Are you ordering enough food for all your people, too?"

"I like the variety." Madero shrugged.

"Same four ingredients."

"Why are you hating? You're Mexican just like me."

"Actually, I'm Spanish. Spaniards have different food."

"Whatever."

• • •

When Madero and Solis pulled into a Taco Bell, Katherine Carter got exactly what she counted on; the two detectives had treated their surveillance detail lightly. It was like they were on her side, helping her win.

She promised herself, and Preston, that as soon as they got rid of the RRs, they would go into hiding again. They were so close. But with pressure from law enforcement increasing, she would have to speed things up to stay one step ahead.

On the drive over to Ellen's house, Katherine weighed her options. The obvious was to take out the tramp herself. With the detectives busy at Taco Bell, she had a small window of opportunity. *What joy it would bring to watch her suffer, to make it clear to her how much she'd hurt my father by making her death an extremely painful one.*

Katherine's other option was to transport Ellen back to her house so Preston could have his way with her—a bit more effort, but doable. She had the tools. Plus, her husband's needs were real. Hers were simply spite. *Decisions, decisions.*

Katherine parked one house down and got out of her Rover. She fondled the retractable baton in her hand on the walk to Ellen's front door. She knew her husband would love it if she brought Ellen to him. Plus, of all the RRs, Ellen was the most deserving of Preston's ways. She would tell him to give that woman extra attention and to draw it out for as long as he could.

She knew all about Ellen's trysts with her father and how she had easily toyed with his emotions. He would often babble about Ellen when he had too much to drink. Katherine didn't understand much at the time, until he started telling her aunt about it. That's when she learned how Ellen had led him to believe she liked him, that she wanted a life together. All she told were filthy lies. Katherine's father died from his drinking, but he also died with a broken heart. That woman tormented her father in his weakest moments, and for that, Katherine wanted to see her punished.

Standing at the front door, Katherine glanced back at the neighborhood. All was quiet. There were no approaching cars or pedestrians nearby. She rang the doorbell and waited.

58

The first thing I noticed when I arrived at the Belle Isle crime scene was the absence of police tape. It was a visual reminder I didn't want to see. I parked a few stalls away from where I remembered Becker's car had been and exited my vehicle. I took a deep breath and surveyed the area. Returning to the crime scene had made my skin prickly.

The walk to the parking spot felt incredibly long. It also didn't help that the emptiness in my stomach felt like a heavy weight. I spent fifteen minutes circling the two stalls where their cars were parked, hoping something on the ground would jump out at me, but nothing had. Even though I had covered the area pretty well, I kept at it.

Stop stalling.

I wasn't ready to face the area where Wilkinson fell. But I had to. It was on the other side of the lot near the grassy edge. I walked until I got to the exact same spot where I had stood that night. Like clockwork, images of Wilkinson lying at my feet flashed across my eyes. I did what I could to flush them from my head, until I realized I needed to see them. I had a case to solve. No matter how hard it got, I had to pull it together. And it got harder, especially when I noticed the reddish-brown stains on the grass. *Wilky, you didn't deserve this.*

When I finished, I let my brain serve up happier thoughts, like Wilkinson driving me around. I immediately let out a burst of laughter, sending a flock of geese grazing nearby off into the winds. I don't know why I thought of that. It irritated him that he had to drive. But he was so cute when he pouted. I had a big smile. I couldn't help it. If he saw me driving a three-hundred horsepower vehicle... Sheesh, the fight we would have had. Honestly, I looked forward to Wilkinson teaching me to drive. I was prepared to fake it.

I removed a tissue from my purse and wiped a tear from my eyes. I liked to think it was a happy cry.

By the time I made it over to the area under the trees, I had regained most of my composure. Being emotional about the situation wouldn't help. The best I could do for Wilkinson was to catch his killer.

I crouched in the spot where I'd left Wilkinson that night. A fair amount of dried leaves and twigs covered most of the ground. I placed my purse down facing the direction where Becker's car would have been and then backed up about ten feet.

Each step I took made a fairly large crunching noise, even with the large lawnmower nearby. There were no trees behind him. No place to hide if someone wanted to. Whoever approached him had to have come up from behind. But if that were the case, he would have heard them, right? He had to have. *What happened, Wilky?*

59

Madero pointed to Ellen Scott's car in her driveway. "See, she's home. We're all good." He pulled his car to the curb opposite the house and parked. "Well, what are you waiting for? Pass me my food."

Madero and Solis dined al fresco in their department-issued car. For twenty minutes, the two men slurped and chomped on the mix and match of four ingredients. Madero came up for air first. "You think we're close to catching the killer? Wait," he held up a hand, "killer*s*?"

Solis shrugged as he always did. It was a tic. "We're certainly making progress. This FBI chick—she knows her stuff."

"Makes you realize how much better we could be at our jobs," Madero said before draining the last of his soda.

"Speak for yourself," Solis shot back.

For the next couple of hours, the detectives continued their discussion on Mexican and Spanish food, which prompted Solis to spend a half hour explaining to Madero how Spaniards were different from Mexicans. They went on to talk about the Detroit Lions and the temperature outside until Madero brought up Agent Kane again.

"Would you fuck her?"

"Kane? Hell, yeah. She's hot. A little short, but I bet she's a spinner," he said, laughing. "What? You wouldn't?"

"Eh. She's got a pretty face and all, but she's too skinny for me. I like big butts. Plus, she's bitchy." Madero remained silent for a few moments. "I'd probably let her blow me."

"You'd *let* her? Sheeeet! Like you got a choice. I can't imagine you turning down anyone who wanted to touch your prick," Solis said, waving off Madero.

"Fuck you."

Another hour passed while Solis and Madero talked about the women they wanted to have sex with. That's when Agent Kane called.

"It's her," Solis said, looking at his cell. "Agent Kane, what can I do for you? Yeah, we're parked right outside her house… She hasn't left since we got here… No, we haven't… We could… Okay, we'll take a look."

"What did she want?"

"She's on her way here but she wants us to check on Ms. Scott, see how she's doing."

Madero shifted in his seat in an effort to exit the car, but Solis stopped him. "Stay here. I got this."

"Fine by me."

Solis got out of the car and crossed the street. He looked up at the sky. The sun had started to set. From the walkway on his way to the door, he could see that the drapes on the front windows were drawn. A quick look around didn't reveal any light from inside the house showing through the uncovered windows. *I wonder if she's in the shower.*

He knocked on the front door and waited fifteen seconds before ringing the bell again, multiple times. He turned back to Madero and shrugged. Again, Solis rang the bell. "Ms. Scott, It's Detective Solis," he called out. "I want to check on you, make sure you're doing okay."

Solis checked the knob on the front door; it was unlocked. He quickly motioned for Madero as he drew his service revolver. A few seconds later, Madero stood next to him.

"She's not responding," Solis said. "Front door is unlocked." Solis slowly pushed the door open while Madero radioed for backup just in case. They didn't want a repeat of what had happened at Belle Isle.

The two detectives entered the living room, guns drawn and pointed in front of them. Solis motioned for Madero to go left while he went right, into the dining room. Everything was neat, not a placemat astray. Solis continued through another doorway and into the kitchen. He placed his hand above the burners of the stove. *Maybe she hasn't eaten yet.* There were no dishes in the sink or half-filled glasses on the counters. He thought it odd that she hadn't snacked on something upon returning home. He exited through another doorway and into a hallway. At the other end, Madero appeared.

"Clear," Madero whispered.

Solis nodded and then pointed up the steps. The barrel of his Smith & Wesson M&P 40 led the way. On the second level, Madero checked the bedroom to the right while Solis kept watch on the hallway.

"Clear," Madero whispered again.

The two made their way down the hall, passing two more rooms and a bathroom. All of the doors were open. One door remained at the end of the hall—the master bedroom.

Backup had yet to arrive, but Solis didn't see any point in waiting. He leaned in and placed his ear against the door, listening for a moment. He heard nothing. Solis held up three fingers and waited for Madero to nod before mouthing a count to three. He grabbed the doorknob and, on three, pushed the door open. They burst into the room with guns out in front. Solis couldn't believe what he saw.

"Shit! It's empty."

Madero walked over to the bathroom. "Where do you think she went?"

"Hell if I know. It doesn't even look like she was here. Nothing in the house looks out of place." Solis holstered his gun and walked over to her dresser. "When people come home from work, they eat or drink something. They head into their bedroom, remove clothing or jewelry… I didn't see any of that."

"Yeah, it's like she parked her car and left. I wonder if there's a basement." A beat later, the two detectives were making their way back down the stairs and looking for the entrance.

"Found it," Solis called out. Madero made his way over to Solis' voice and saw him standing in front of an open door, looking at steps.

Solis flipped the light switch at the top of the stairs and headed down. "Basement looks finished." Madero followed him. When Solis reached the bottom, he turned to the right and stopped.

"What?" Madero asked. "She got bad taste?" When he reached the bottom, he, too, stopped dead in his tracks.

60

Blood was everywhere.

The walls. The carpet. The pool table. Nothing was spared. The thick and sticky had pooled, splattered, and dripped.

Ellen Scott lay naked, face up on the pool table, her pale skin smeared with blood. Her scalp, completely removed, hung on the light fixture above the table. Each arm and leg pointed to a corner pocket. Between her legs, pool balls were clustered, as if spilling from her vagina. Peeking out was the cue ball. Later, they would discover more inside of her. Solis let out a big breath as he ran his hand through his hair.

For the first time in a long time, Madero shot a look of concern to his partner. "What are we going to tell her?"

A moment later, they heard the doorbell ring.

• • •

I stood there defeated. It felt as if someone had ripped out my insides. The loss of Ellen Scott was unthinkable, and yet it had happened. Blood covered the entire basement. Rage was the motivator. I walked around the table, letting my eyes detail the scene. The body reminded me of a case I had seen back in Hong Kong. The victim had been severely tortured and then killed by *Ling Chi*, death by one thousand cuts.

Ellen's face had been scored like a piece of meat. Her arms, legs, and torso all suffered multiple lacerations as well. At closer inspection, I noticed the necessary incisions to the carotid and the femoral artery. *Why the disfigurement though? This wasn't the killer's M.O.* I turned to Solis and Madero after I finished. "Which one of you wants to explain first?"

It took Solis fifteen minutes to walk me through what they did from the moment they left me to follow Ellen.

"So let me see if I understand this correctly. After I told you to stick with Ms. Scott, you two proceeded to pull into a Taco Bell drive-thru—"

Madero started. "Look, it wasn't—"

"Wasn't what? I told you to stick with her, and you didn't. Then, when you arrive here, you don't bother to do a house search? For all we know, the killer could have been waiting for her to get home."

I threw my arms up in the air, disgusted at the sheer level of incompetence these two men displayed. We had been making progress. I stopped my muttering and pacing and faced them. "Ellen could have already been dead by the time you two parked your fat asses outside. Think about that."

"We were ten, maybe fifteen minutes behind her," Solis offered.

"Look around. This guy is good at what he does. I don't think he needs much time." I walked around the basement and then pointed to some stained carpeting. "The blood coagulated and is starting to thicken. It's very sticky over here on the table. It looks like she was killed soon after she got home. If you were with her and checked the house before letting her in, this might have been prevented."

I can't believe I trusted those guys. I can't believe I thought I could. I should have escorted Ellen Scott back home, checked the house, and then gone down to Belle Isle. *Woulda, shoulda, coulda.*

The fact of the matter was, I still needed these guys. I couldn't do it alone, and I didn't want Reilly sending out an army of field agents. It was my case. "Look, guys. We need to regroup and pull together. We had a setback. What's done is done."

The three of us worked alongside CSI the entire night. We were bound to find something if we looked hard enough. That, I wanted to believe.

61

The next day Lieutenant White wanted to talk about the case. I wasn't so sure I wanted to talk to him. To top it off, he asked me to meet him at the Woodward Dream Cruise instead of at his office. *Great.*

I looked it up on the Internet and discovered that it was a parade of old cars that drove up and down Woodward Avenue at three miles per hour. Apparently, it was a weeklong event, and people lined up on the sidewalk to watch. *Oh, the excitement.*

White said to meet him at Roy's Custom Detailing at the corner of Vester and Woodward. *Next time I'll suggest the makeup counter at Macy's.*

When I reached the location, I spotted White right away. He had on a brightly colored aloha shirt and white shorts. *This is what happens when people who are used to wearing uniforms find they have to wear something else.*

The organization he was with, some car aficionado club, had a pretty nice setup for guests to watch the cars cruise by. Lots of shady space and chairs, something I appreciated since it was another blistering day.

"Agent Kane, thanks for meeting me here." White stuck his hand out and smiled.

I shook his hand and smiled back. "I can see why you wanted to meet here. The cars look great," I said, looking around, feigning interest.

"Something to drink? Beer? Soda? Bottled water?"

"Water would be nice."

White dug into the cooler filled with a slushy mixture of cans and bottles. A moment later he pulled a bottle of water out. "Here you go. Ice cold." White motioned to a chair on the sidewalk. "Have a seat, Agent."

I sat and took a few sips of water, careful not to give myself brain freeze.

"I heard about the latest victim." White was direct, probably because he wanted to get back to looking at old cars and scaring small children with his outfit. He held up his hand and counted down with his fingers. "The Walters, Rick Tanner, Archie Becker, that reporter, and now Ellen Scott. Throw in your partner and that's a total of seven on your watch."

I couldn't believe what I was hearing. I thought maybe the sound of the engines revving in my right ear had distorted what he said, but when I inquired again, it sounded the same. He blamed me for those deaths. I nearly exploded at him but kept my tongue buried. "With all due respect, Lieutenant, I'm not responsible for those deaths. I'm investigating this case and working to catch the killer as fast as I can."

"The newspapers are having a field day with this."

"Lieutenant White, is this why you called me down here, to tell me how many people have died? Because it's a waste of my time; I already knew the answer."

"We're getting a lot of pressure from the top, not to mention calls from the big three. They're losing their executive talent."

I had no interest in getting into a point-the-finger battle with White. *He's doing what he's doing: being a distraction.*

"Look, Lieutenant, I appreciate your concerns. I've noted them. Now if that's all you had to discuss—thank you for the cold drink and I'll update you when I have something."

Before I could stand, a smiling man approached us. He had a cocky smirk that he wanted to pass off as a smile.

"You must be Agent Kane."

He knows my name? Should I know his? I don't recall seeing him in the briefing or ever meeting him. "Yes, I am." I extended my hand. For a quick second, it looked as if he were going to kiss it but had second thoughts. Thank God for second thoughts. "Have we met before?"

Lieutenant White spoke then. "Agent Kane, this is Stevie Roscoe. He's the chief of staff for the mayor of Detroit."

Mayor? How does he know me and why is he talking to me? "Mr. Roscoe, I wasn't aware we would be meeting. I'm sorry if I look surprised."

"Please, call me Stevie," he said through his smile. "You're probably wondering how I know about you. It's my job. You're the hotshot agent sent out here to rid us of our problem."

"You mean the two psychos running round slashing throats?"

"Two?"

I smiled and looked over at White and then back at Stevie. "Didn't you know? We discovered there are two of them. They work in a team, and that's why they've eluded capture for so long." I dragged out the word "long" to see how he would react. *Did he know about the cover-up?*

"I did not know that."

I barely knew the guy, but I already didn't like him. His demeanor didn't sit right in my gut. Icky seemed to describe it best.

"Well, I assume you're getting close to capturing this duo, with your highly praised background and all."

What was with these people? They all seemed to be preoccupied with pointing out my background with a sense of ill regard. Never before had I met a bunch of city officials who needed so much help but made the help feel so unwanted. "Like I told Lieutenant White, we're making progress. I have to get back to work." I stood up and smiled at the two men before turning and leaving.

62

In my opinion, wearing sweats was the best way to get work done. I headed straight back to my hotel. There, I had air conditioning, as much green tea as I could possibly want, and silence. Oh, and chocolate.

The humidity had taken its toll on me. I was halfway through the lobby, mentally undressing, when my phone alerted me to a text. I hoped it wasn't White. I'd have to ignore him. It wasn't. It was Lucy.

"hi mommy," the text read.

"Hi, Lucy. Mommy loves you."

I waited for a response during the ride up to the fourteenth floor, but none came. *Hmm, weird.* As soon as I entered my room, I peeled off my slightly damp shirt and jeans, unhooked my bra, and settled into a fresh T-shirt, avoiding my sweatpants for now. I checked my phone once again. Still no text from Lucy. Must have been a text-by.

A moment later, my phone rang and I picked it up, thinking Lucy decided to call.

"Agent Kane, this is Agent Ton. We spoke a few weeks ago."

"Yes, of course. What can I do for you?"

"Did you still need information on those surviving hostages from the bank robbery?"

"Anything would be of help." I sat down at the room desk and grabbed a pen. "Go ahead."

"One of the hostages is a professor at Oakland University."

I wrote it down. "Where is that?"

"Auburn Hills. Do you know the area?"

"I've been there once. What's his name?"

"All I have is a first name. It's Preston."

Preston. Not a typical name, I thought. "What about the other hostage?"

"Nothing yet, but if something comes up, I'll get a hold of you."

"Can I reach you at the number you're calling on?"

"I prefer you didn't. Like I said, if I get my hands on any new information, I'll get a hold of you." He then hung up.

I looked at the name I'd written on the notepad. *All right, Preston. What can you tell me?*

63

Located near the center of the Oakland University campus was the unmistakable mirrored building named O'Dowd Hall. Preston Carter had spent a large part of his life in the building, teaching students the ins and outs of biology. His students liked him for his open-door policy and his hands-on approach to teaching. They said he didn't teach them—he showed them.

On the second floor, about thirty students had their heads lowered as they crafted the perfect essay answers. Some mumbled, while others took moments to ponder in between sentences. The class was human biology, Preston's favorite to teach. It was also his last class for the day, so he had already mentally checked out.

He sat quietly in a corner, tapping away on his laptop, occasionally glancing up at the class to make sure eyes didn't stray from their own papers. Preston couldn't stand cheating, mostly because he didn't understand why someone would cheat in his class. It was such an interesting subject. How could one not want to know that stuff? The students seemed focused. Thirty pens were scratching across paper, so he went back to his hobby.

Preston scrolled across a map of Corktown. That's

where it all started. He loved Google Maps. It was the perfect way to reminisce. He absolutely loved retracing his steps and re-familiarizing himself with the areas. And with street view, he could literally reenact a kill. How special.

The rattle of plastic rang out from the cheap timer sitting on a counter next to him. "Pens down, everyone," he said, looking up briefly. "If you haven't answered the questions by now, you don't know the answer."

One by one, the students got up from their seats with their belongings and made their way to the front of the room, where they placed their exams on the desk.

"Please go over Chapters 42 and 43," Preston called out. "We will be discussing them in our next class. Also, bring your lab tools with you." He didn't bother to look up from his laptop that time. Not until he heard someone call his first name—a big no-no for students.

64

I had to wait until Monday to track down the professor, but it didn't take long to pin down the name Agent Ton fed me once I got to the university. He was Preston Carter, professor of biology, and the class I was about to enter was his last one for the day. Rather than interrupt, I waited in the hallway. The students looked as if they were taking an exam. School was important, and college was expensive. If my kid had his test interrupted by someone like me, I'd be pissed.

In the meantime, I got to talk with Lucy via text. I answered ten "why" questions in a row. My favorite was why she shouldn't fart in class to draw attention to herself. Now that's a call every parent looks forward to receiving from their child's school. Even though I enjoyed the texting with Lucy, I hated being away. Last night, Lucy had cried throughout our entire phone conversation. It tore at my heart and pissed me off at the same time. I looked at my phone for another 'why' question but none came. We were done talking.

A chime sounded, and students poured into the hallway a few seconds later. I entered Professor Carter's classroom after the last person walked out. It looked like your typical school lab—long rows of black countertop tables with mixing faucets and gas cock valves. There were fish tanks filled with sea anemones and glass cupboards packed with jars housing dead mammals.

I thought for a second the professor might have slipped out with the students, but then I spotted a man in the corner sitting in a student's chair. It looked two sizes too small. He seemed to be really occupied with his laptop, because he didn't hear me clear my throat.

"Preston… Preston Carter?"

The blond man looked up from his laptop. His forehead wrinkled as his eyes sharpened their look on me. "Yes, that's me. Do I know you?"

I pulled out my badge as I walked over to him. "I'm Agent Kane, FBI. I'd like to ask you a few questions. Do you have a moment?"

"What is this about? Did one of my students get into trouble?"

"No, it's about you. If my information is correct, you were one of the two surviving hostages in the Comerica Bank hold-up seven years ago."

He let out a noisy breath before slamming his laptop closed. "Look, I spent hours answering questions for the authorities back then. All I want to do is forget and move on, and I can't do that if you guys keep coming back to ask the same questions over and over," he said in a raised voice. I watched the color on his face grow warm and his lips press tighter together.

"Has someone else come by recently to question you?"

The professor was agitated. He ran his hand through his hair continually. "I know they were watching me. They didn't believe what I said, so they watched me. Guess what? Nothing. I was telling the truth."

Had I known he would get upset over a few questions, I would have brought a shiny red apple. "I know this is difficult but it would be extremely helpful for me—"

"You! How is this helpful? They solved the case. The man is behind bars. What exactly are you doing?"

I'm investigating a crime, a-hole. I gritted my teeth. "First off, I'm asking the questions. Your only job is to answer it. It's like a test. You know what a test is, right?"

His head jerked back. The professor wasn't expecting that answer.

"We believe the man arrested was not responsible for all the murders that took place at that bank robbery or any of the murders that happened beforehand. You were there, Professor. Did you see Michael Garrison kill all those people?"

His shoulders relaxed and his voice calmed as he gave in to my questioning. "Yes, he killed them. He shot them. So did his girlfriend."

"Girlfriend? She killed some of the hostages?"

"Sure. She killed two bank tellers."

That was news. Nowhere in the investigation notes did

I see mention of the girlfriend killing anyone. Nor did I recall any mention of another gun. "Why did he kill his girlfriend?"

"I don't know," he said, shrugging. "The man didn't appear to have all his marbles. I sensed he was bipolar. Okay one minute—batty the next."

"What about the victims that had their throats slashed? Did you see Mr. Garrison kill those people?"

He threw his arms up in the air. "Of course I did. We all did. The man was a psycho."

I kept my professional composure, but inside I felt like someone had just socked me in the stomach. Could Garrison have been lying to me that day we spoke? If so, that would mean Detroit had captured the right guy. And I needed to catch a copycat. How could my instincts on the case have been so, so wrong?

I stared absent-mindedly at my notebook, trying to comprehend what the professor had just told me. It was gut wrenching to say the least.

"Well, if that's all the questions you have. I must be going." The professor stood up and walked over to his desk to gather his things. I was still lost in a confusing haze as I followed him. He put his laptop into his briefcase. When he slipped his brown sport coat on, something metallic slipped out and landed near my shoe. I bent down and picked up a single Mercedes key on a key holder. I looked up at the professor, realizing for the first time his height and his long blond hair that reached his shoulders.

He stared back at me and held out his hand. "Thank you."

I looked at the key I held and then back at him before asking what kind of Mercedes he drove.

65

"Excuse me?" Preston asked, accentuating the wrinkles in his forehead.

"Your Mercedes. What model do you have?"

He gazed at me a bit longer with his confused look before shaking it off and snatching the keys out of my hand. Before he turned away, I grabbed him by the arm. "Professor, I asked you a question."

He looked back at me with a smile. A moment later, the back of his hand connected with the side of my head. The force sent me flying through the air like a china doll. I landed on a lab table and then rolled off onto the floor. It happened so fast. My head ached and my equilibrium was off, making the room tilt to the side. I sat down and closed my eyes for a few seconds. When I opened them, I felt better and could stand again. I forged ahead, out of the classroom and into the hallway. It was empty save for a few students.

"Where did he go?" I called out. "Professor Carter, did anybody see him?"

"He went down the stairs," a student called out.

"Are you okay?" another asked, coming up to me.

I brushed him off and headed down the stairs as

quickly as my legs could muster. When I reached the bottom, most of my senses had returned, and moving had gotten easier. I exited the building only to be faced with a large campus full of crisscrossing students, and the professor was nowhere to be seen. He may have escaped, but I knew who our killer was.

I quickly put in a call to Detective Solis. "Detective, it's Agent Kane. I've identified one of the killers." I told him where I was and why I had come in search of the professor.

"You were right," he said. "One of the surviving hostages *was* the other killer at the bank."

"Had to be, or why would the professor run? We got a name. It should be easy to track down an address."

"I'm on it," Solis said.

"We need to be careful of how we take Preston Carter down."

"I'll get the tactical unit involved and start preparations. Still can't believe the nickname for the hostage had stuck. If that's the case, the other hostage should be a student."

"I doubt that person is still a student today," I said.

"You're probably right about that. I wonder if they knew each other or if it was just coincidence."

"Well there are two killers, so my guess is there were two back then. I think it's safe to say they knew each other." Preston must have thought a mind was a terrible thing to waste.

66

I met up with Solis and Madero back at central precinct. It didn't take long for them to get an address on the guy. At first, I didn't make the connection until they mentioned the Corktown neighborhood. Preston Carter was married to Katherine Carter, the beautiful brunette Wilkinson and I had talked to a few weeks ago. I had her pegged as an intelligent woman with her life together. I guess I was wrong. Maybe Preston was really smarter than he appeared. *A sicko with a wife and kids... How is it she has no idea what her husband was up to? Or did she?*

I've come across my fair share of husbands who led secret lives, but Preston Carter took the cake. The wives always swore they knew nothing. "How could we know?" they would say. *How could you not?*

With the latest information, the situation had escalated. Not only did we need to take the professor down, but we also needed to make sure we got the wife and kids out of the house and into our custody before he did something stupid, like take them hostage. I also had to make sure she wasn't a part of it. We knew there were two. I needed them both in custody and separated, in case Katherine was innocent. I didn't want to jeopardize her or the kids by having them in a place where Preston could get to them.

Within two hours, we had mobilized a block away from the Carter's residence. We had sent a team ahead inside a cable van to survey the property. Our suspect had not returned home yet, but they reported the wife had just returned with the two kids. It would be a perfect time to grab her and the kids and remove them from the picture.

Solis handed me a flak jacket with the word "police" stenciled on the back. "You might want to put this on."

We were following the tactical team in the front door. Madero entered the house from behind with the rest of the team.

We got into our position, crouching near a hedge in the front of the house and out of sight of the front door. A member of the team dressed as a cable guy approached the house. A few moments after Katherine answered the door, we got the signal and everyone mobilized on the house. We had the home cleared and Katherine and her two children in an SUV on their way to a safe location all in under five minutes.

I rode with Katherine and the kids. The youngest cried the entire time, and Katherine kept asking what was happening and insisted on calling her husband; we had confiscated her cell. I dreaded having to tell her. It wasn't a good idea to have that conversation in front of her children. I told her that, as soon as we got to our location, I would explain everything and answer all her questions.

I insisted Lieutenant White secure clearance for a suite at the hotel I had been staying at. Any place but Central Precinct would do for now. I didn't think we could keep them safe at Central, mainly because I trusted no one there. Preston was too good and too smart. Plus, I wanted to keep Katherine close by. She would be key to catching Preston.

• • •

It didn't take long for Katherine to put the boys down for a nap; the experience had them worn out. She closed the door to the bedroom and took a seat in the sitting area next to me. Solis and Madero were also in the hotel room.

Katherine looked frightened. I could see it in her eyes, but she tried hard to hide it. Though she had no idea what was coming her way, she was about to find out who she really married.

"Did something happen to Preston? Is he… dead?"

"No," I answered. "We don't know where your husband is, but it's important we find him. Katherine, there's no right way to say this, so I'm just going to say it. Preston is a suspect in the rash of recent murders."

"What?" Katherine reeled back. "You have got to be kidding me." A half smile appeared on her face but disappeared quickly when no one answered her.

"You're serious, aren't you?"

"We are," I said. "Katherine, your husband attacked me this afternoon when I tried to question him at the university." I pulled my hair back and showed her the bruising near my ear.

"Preston is not a violent man. Are you sure you haven't mistaken someone else for him?"

Solis removed a picture of Preston from an envelope. "Is this your husband?"

Katherine took a moment before nodding and answering yes.

"If he's innocent, like you say he is, then he shouldn't have a problem," I said.

"Well, what do you want me to do?"

I handed Katherine her cell phone. "You can start by calling him."

Katherine tried four times and got voicemail with each call. "Please, honey, call me when you get this. It's important. I love you."

I reached over and gently took the phone from her hands. She didn't resist me. "Think, Katherine. Where would your husband go?"

Katherine shook her head back and forth slowly.

"It's okay. Take your time," I said. We already had units watching the house and his office at the campus. I wasn't holding my breath, though.

Suddenly, her eyes shot upward to the left. She'd thought of something.

"What is it? What did you just remember?"

She was hesitant, so I gently held her hand. "You want to help your husband don't you?"

"He often likes to drive along Lake St. Clair."

I remembered the gazebo Wilkinson had shown me.

"Anything else? What about a friend's place? Where does he hang out?" Knowing Preston was working with someone else, we had to be careful.

"Preston doesn't have many friends. Lots of colleagues."

"Are any of them close to him?"

Katherine thought for moment. "Professor Burroughs, they've known each other for over twenty years."

"Does he work at the same university?"

She shook her head. "He works at the Macomb campus for Oakland Community College, though I think Preston mentioned that he might have retired."

I wonder if this Burroughs guy is the other killer.

Madero got on the phone and started hunting down an address. I motioned for Solis to bring in the uniforms that were waiting outside. They would be providing security while the three of us headed out to the lake.

I turned to Katherine. "You'll be safe here with these officers."

"Safe from what?" she asked, shaking her head, confused.

"Safe from your husband."

• • •

Not wanting to hang out with the police, Katherine retired to the bedroom, locking the door behind her. The boys were still napping on the king-size bed. She stared at them lovingly for a moment before kicking off her shoes and taking a seat on the bed. Figuring she was stuck, she decided to join them and rest for a bit. *Might as well make the best of it*, she thought.

But first, she gently turned the little one, Jackson, over to his side. She reached down the front of his shorts and revealed a hidden pocket sewn inside. The police were quick to pat her down and confiscate her cell phone, not so much with the little ones. She, of course, had a hunch they wouldn't frisk her children.

She removed the tiny, no-frills cell phone and lay next to him. She had a plan, of course, in the event of something like that happening. Thanks to Katherine's neurotic ways, she had prepared the family for a variety of scenarios.

After Preston ran out of O'Dowd Hall, he called his wife and gave her the heads up about the FBI agent wanting to question him. "Surely they are on the way to the house if they're not already there," he told her.

Luckily, when Preston called, Katherine happened to be on the road, having just picked up the boys from school. She pulled off the freeway and drove into the parking lot of a mall, making her way to the top floor of the parking structure. She removed a bag from the side storage compartment of the vehicle. Inside were the boys' special clothing.

Lorenzo and Jackson knew exactly what to do. They

had practiced the drill many times. Katherine and the boys were ready by the time they returned home. All she had to do was sit in her favorite chair and wait for the knock at the door.

Holed up in protective custody, it was time for another plan to go into effect. The grin on Katherine's face grew wider as she turned on the phone and sent Preston a text.

67

The three of us had already started to drip again during our short walk to the car. I badly wanted to peel off my clothes. "Solis, call whoever you need to increase the number of patrols along the lake. We might get lucky."

A second later, the beeping and ringing of various cellphones could be heard. All three of us patted our pockets to take our calls.

"Solis here. Yes, of course. How are you Mrs. Tanner?"

"Tanner?" I mouthed to Madero.

"Rick Tanner, the engineer," he said.

Everything clicked. She was out of town when we found her husband.

Solis hung up. "That was Mrs. Tanner. She remembered a realtor had stopped by the house the day she left town. Might be something. I told her to take a picture of the lady's card and email it to me."

I turned to Madero. I felt sorry for the big guy. He had rings under his arms the size of hula hoops.

"My guy's coming up empty on Burroughs at OCC. He's still working on a home address."

I wondered if she had lied.

The two detectives continued to look at me quietly. They were waiting for a report on my phone call. "Oh, that was Lucy texting me."

On the drive to the lake, I thought about my hunch—that Katherine was lying. Why would she though? As a mother of two children, the most important thing to her would be their safety. If there were any chance her husband was dangerous, she should want to know.

I thought about her father, Eddie Bass. Was he a good dad? Katherine was just a little girl when he died, but she seemed to speak highly of him. Probably loved him unconditionally up until the day he drank himself to death, even though it agitated her when I brought it up that day we questioned her. Could she have lied about knowing what her father knew? She said she had no idea who the RRs were. But what if she lied about that, too? What if everything she said to date was a lie? What if—

My God! Katherine is the other part of the team!

68

"It's her," I said. "Turn the car around."

Solis looked back at me. "Huh?"

"Katherine," I said. "She's the other part of the team! She has to be. Her father admits to knowing about the RRs. Ellen Scott admitted to knowing Katherine's father."

"Didn't she say she had never heard of them when you questioned her?" Solis asked.

"She did. She said her father never mentioned them. But what if she lied about everything she's told us to date just like she could be lying about Professor Burroughs? I turned to Madero. "Your guy just called to say he came up empty."

He nodded in agreement.

"Think about it. If her father told her about the RRs and Ellen Scott, she could theoretically blame them for her father's death. She wanted revenge."

"So you're saying she did all the killing?"

"She would definitely be involved with the deaths of the RRs. I'm not sure about the other victims dating back to the very first one found in Corktown. Obviously Katherine wasn't married to Preston back then. He's the true killer. He killed all those people."

"You saying this lady fell in love with a serial killer?" Madero added.

"Why not? Women do stupid things when they're in love. Maybe she didn't know at first, or maybe she had a hunch but made up excuses—"

"Like an abused spouse."

"Exactly. Or maybe she's just as screwed up as him and has desires but is able to control them. Some killers can do that. I don't think Preston is one of them, though; the urge would be too strong for him but her—she's different. I think she's the brains behind the operation."

Madero flipped a switch, and the cry of the siren did its job as cars peeled off the road ahead of us. Solis called the two uniforms watching Katherine and her boys. "I'm not getting any answer from either one."

My hunch told me they were already dead and Katherine was gone. But how often is my hunch right? It warned me earlier. "Madero, how much longer to the hotel?"

"Fifteen minutes."

She seemed so normal. She was a mother like me. But the more I thought about it, the more I believed it. Katherine was the matriarch of that twisted family business. She knew how to control her husband. Not only did she feed his need, she fed hers.

・・・

We exited the elevator and hurried down the hallway.

A uniform exited the room just as we got there. He shook his head. "Both officers are down. The woman and the children are gone."

Right away, I noticed the blood against the white backdrop of the suite. The first body was slumped over a white linen couch. Another uniform exited the bedroom, pointing back. "The other one is in there."

I walked over to the bedroom. Lying in a pool of blood soaked carpet next to the left side of the bed was the second officer. Both had their neck slashed. *How did she pull this off? How? She had two kids with her. Is this the new definition of supermom?*

I walked back into the sitting area, shaking my head.

Solis threw out a theory. "Okay, maybe she lures one of our guys into the bedroom—her kid's sick or something like that. He bends down to check out the kid, that's when she comes up behind him and slashes his neck."

"You were the one who frisked her. Did you miss the knife?"

Solis shrugged, realizing the hole in his theory.

"Even if she somehow got rid of one in the room," I motioned, "I find it hard to believe she overpowered the second one. He would have been looking right at her as she exited the room."

"Maybe she had help," Madero added.

"Preston," I said.

"How? We disconnected the phone in the room and

confiscated her cell phone."

Thinking back to my supermom thought, what would she do? She was the brain of the family; she would have planned for this. Would she have used her children? "Were the children searched?"

Solis and Madero looked at each other before looking back at me. I already knew their answer.

"She used her kids. She must have—probably hid stuff on them like a cellphone or even a weapon. She took a chance they wouldn't get searched. She then gets a hold of Preston, tells him where they are, and they orchestrated a double killing."

"Everyone has an ID on Preston. They wouldn't just open the door and let him waltz right in," Solis said.

I stood quietly for moment, wondering how I would use my kids to get out of that situation. "Okay, I'm riffing here, but assume Katherine figured out a good reason to get one of the officers into the bedroom. He enters and the two kids exit at the same time. One immediately runs over to the other officer to distract him while the other runs to the door to open it."

I walked over to the door to the room. "Solis, pretend you're the officer; you're sitting on the couch."

Solis walked over to the couch and sat down.

"Okay now, you see the little boy run to the door. You get up to stop him, but before you can, the other boy jumps on you to play. While you're trying to pry this boy off of you, the other one opens the door."

"Should I stand up?" Solis asked.

"What would you do if a little boy jumped on you?"

"I'd pull him off and stop the other from opening the door."

"Okay, you get the kid off of you fairly quickly. You stand up and make your way over to the door, but the other boy opens it before you reach him. In comes Preston. Before you can respond or draw your weapon, he's moved across the room."

I walked to where the blood splatter first appeared on the carpeting. "This is where he cuts you and pushes you back, still attacking until you fall on the couch, bleeding to death. In the meantime, she deals with the uniform in the room."

"That's a lot of assumption," Madero said, "but it seems plausible if she actually coached her kids to play a role in her sick game."

"Never underestimate a mother's ability to make everyone fall into line."

The two detectives flashed me a look of confusion.

"She's supermom. She cooks, cleans, raises the kids, and plans the murders. She coached them—trust me."

Solis' phone beeped. He pulled it out of the hip holster he wore and punched a few buttons. "Got the photo of the Realtor's card." He turned his phone around. The person smiling on the card was Katherine Carter.

69

The worst had just happened. Katherine and Preston had gone into hiding. That doubled my worry lines; they were extremely good at disappearing. They were the type that hid in plain view, but you wouldn't know it until you found them. That's how they avoided capture the first time around. *What's the saying? If it ain't broke?*

If Reilly got wind of it, I knew all bets would be off, and a convention of agents would descend on Detroit. I didn't want that. The fighting, stubborn, and hardheaded side of me wanted the case all to myself.

Obviously Katherine had plans for her family to disappear when we showed up at the house. With Ellen Scott finally dead, she had reached her goal of eliminating all five RRs. She'd had her revenge.

But what about Preston?

His brain was wired to kill. It had needs and there was no changing that. I doubt he had the desire or the means necessary to stop cold turkey and turn into a simple soccer dad. From my knowledge, cold-blooded killers like Preston didn't work that way. They couldn't contain their wants. How on earth would Katherine keep him under control? How did she do it in the past? Katherine had proven back in that room that she could not only kill, but she could orchestrate a plan to kill. I batted the thought around before striking another aha moment.

"She feeds him," I blurted out.

Solis and Madero looked at me.

"She's feeding him victims. That's how she keeps him under control."

Solis scratched the back of his head. "You mean like an animal, with scheduled feedings and all?"

"Yes. Like any woman, she knows her man better than he knows himself."

Madero rolled his eyes.

"Trust me, men have pretty simple desires. It's not hard to control someone when you know what buttons to press."

Solis shrugged. "I'll bite. So you're saying she knew how long he could go without a kill before he went apeshit?"

"That's exactly what I'm saying. Days, weeks… maybe a month. She had to know. Preston was a dangerous man. In a dire situation, he would take one of them if he had to."

"But she wouldn't let that happen, right?" Solis asked.

"No, she would never put the two boys in a situation where she couldn't protect them. Plus, she's a control freak. I bet no one in the family made a move without her knowing about it—better yet, allowing it."

"So she feeds him," Solis repeated.

I shifted my weight from heel to heel. "Even though they've gone underground, Preston won't stop killing. Somehow, they're able to keep doing it without anyone knowing."

The detectives stared at me.

"She needs easy prey," I said, breaking the silence. "A bountiful supply of victims. Where would she get them?"

"Runaways," Solis said.

"Drug addicts, prostitutes," Madero continued.

I snapped my finger. "That's it. Easy. Plentiful. And the best part: no one will miss them if they go missing."

But what did they do with the bodies? I had a hunch the Carter residence held our answer.

70

Madero proved to be helpful by securing a search warrant in under an hour from a friendly judge. Our plan was to toss every square inch of that house. I didn't care if Katherine was supermom; everyone makes mistakes. I was banking on it.

Solis and Madero started on the main level. I headed upstairs, straight for the master bedroom. I wanted to know how Mr. and Mrs. Serial Killer lived.

They had a typical room. It was spacious, with wall-to-wall carpet and a custom walk-in closet with built-ins. In the center of the room, a king-size bed had half a dozen throw pillows neatly arranged on it. Off to either side were a couple of sitting chairs. The en suite had a separate bath and shower, dual vanity, and a toilet. So far, nothing stood out as odd. Except Preston had more hair product than any man should be allowed to have.

Katherine had a separate makeup vanity in the corner of the room. I sat on the crushed-velvet seat and skimmed the top of the table. Everything was neat and in its place. Nothing uncapped, uncovered or unscrewed—the complete opposite of my bathroom counter. She was so perfect.

Her taste in makeup was a little of everything. Her

jewelry was nice—not out of this world, but Preston had been generous. Katherine owned one bottle of perfume, Chanel. I remembered smelling it on her when we first met.

In the walk-in closet, I half-expected to find something creepy, something that screamed "horror couple." But I didn't. She even had great taste in lingerie. I closed the drawer and made my way to the end table near the bed. I could tell she slept on the right. The left side had a larger dent in the bed.

I opened the tiny drawer. *Customized woodwork.* I noticed the pink rabbit first. *Sheesh, how much more perfectly boring and stereotypical could they be? They killed people for Godsake.*

I grabbed a tissue from a box on the table and used it to push aside the toy. Under a few pieces of paper, I discovered a tiny leather-bound booklet. Using another tissue, I removed it from the drawer and flipped the cover open.

Bingo!

71

Written inside the book were dates going back at least five years. Next to each date, in the same neat penmanship, were GPS coordinates. *What have you been up to, Katherine?*

I headed to the basement where Solis and Madero were. "I found something interesting," I said.

"So did we," Solis replied. He and Madero were standing next to a butcher-block table large enough in size that Madero could lay on it.

Solis pointed to the four corners. "Fasteners. One could easily strap someone down to this table if they wanted."

I took a closer look. The wood looked weathered, like it had been washed over and over. There were small chips and nicks around the edges. Lastly, there were hundreds of shallow grooves on the surface I could only imagine were left by the tools of Preston's trade. *His man cave?* "Well, we know where they made their kills while hiding."

Solis pointed to my hand. "What's that?"

I opened the notebook and flipped through it, showing Solis and Madero the dates and the coordinates.

"How far back does it go?" Solis asked.

"At least five years. There must be hundreds of

entries."

Solis scratched at his chin. "And each entry has a different location attached?"

"Looks like it."

"My money says this is where they buried bodies. If they killed them here, they still had to deal with the disposal of the bodies."

"Why don't we look behind curtain number one?" Madero said, pointing to a large padlocked storage. "I got bolt cutters in my car. I'll be right back."

Solis flipped through the pages of the notebook. "That's a lot of bodies. Why would they keep track of where they buried them?"

"It's about keeping order. I'm guessing each body has its own private plot. Neat and orderly."

"Only one way to find out for sure," Solis said, holding the notebook up. "Follow the coordinates."

Madero returned with the bolt cutters. One grunt later and the lock landed on the cement floor with a thud. We all stared at the freezer, wondering who would open it. Finally Madero straightened his jacket and stepped forward. He grabbed the door with both hands and lifted up.

"What the hell is that?" he said.

72

After hearing Madero's reaction, Solis and I reluctantly took a step forward. Inside, there were five or six clear plastic bags filled with frozen red goop. It's the best way I could explain it.

Madero lifted up a bag. With overhead light hitting the bag, it was easier to decipher the contents; the bag contained at least one arm. But what stood out the most was that it had been sliced into quarter-inch-thick slices like a piece of salami.

We picked through the other bags. Each one had mostly recognizable body parts made up of frozen slices.

Madero motioned to a band saw against the other wall. "Now we know what the big saw is for."

"They do this in research," Solis said. "I saw a documentary on TV where a serial killer left his body to science. They froze the body and would slice it up like this, except they were slivers, almost transparent horizontal cuts through the body to study."

"I think I saw that one," Madero chimed in. "They could cut thousands of slices from the brain and give it to other researchers, right?"

"Yeah that's the one. What's the guy's name?"

"I dunno, but he was a crazy killer. It was a huge coup to get him to say yes."

So quickly I lose them. "I hate to break up this feel-good party the two of you are experiencing, but could we focus?"

A quick count gave us five bags total. The victim was female—the carved-out breasts gave it away. My best guess is the Carters hadn't had time to get rid of the body. Madero called it in while Solis and I continued to poke at the bags.

"I'm guessing this victim was one of Preston's scheduled feedings. When he's done, they slice them up, bag them, and freeze them until they can get them buried."

"Unless someone's sifting for bone fragments, they would never know a body was there once it decomposed," Solis added.

I held up the notebook in my hand. "I bet this is private land. There might even be a cabin on the property."

A siren whirring followed by tires screeching grabbed our attention. "Sounds like the gang's here."

Madero led the way up and briefed the uniforms as they entered the house. I could hear him telling the sergeant to get a perimeter set up. He also asked for the ETA on the forensics team. I felt a tap on my shoulder.

"Agent Kane, I bet you have a GPS navigator in your rental," Solis said with a raised eyebrow.

Before I could answer, Madero appeared.

"The sergeant on duty passed on a message. Lieutenant

White is on the way. Doesn't want us to go anywhere until he gets here."

"That's too bad," I said. "We got a case to solve."

73

The three of us piled into my rental and we drove north on I-75. Solis opened up the booklet and punched in the coordinates of the most recent date logged. The area was up north, in the sticks, as they say. Solis tried a few more coordinates, and they all came up in the same vicinity, an area on the north side of Loon Lake. According to my talking GPS unit, it would take three hours to get there.

I had time to think during the drive. My partner entered my thoughts, again. When I realized Katherine was the other killer, I knew she had killed Wilkinson that night. I'm sure she didn't hide her approach. She probably knew he would be confused to see her there. His defenses would be down. That's how she got the jump on him that night. He was a sitting target and didn't even know it.

"What's the plan?" Solis asked. "There are four of them and three of us."

He counted the children. "We should assume Katherine might have more tricks up her sleeve. Let's not underestimate them."

Madero cleared his throat. "Are we trying to apprehend them or put an end to this?"

"What do you mean?" I asked, glancing back at him

through the rearview mirror.

"Well, assuming they're armed and dangerous. Taking them alive might be more difficult than taking them out."

I didn't need to think my answer over. The two had killed a lot of innocent people, including Wilkinson. "We take no chances."

My phone chimed, signaling I had a text message.

"You want me to check that? Might be important," Solis said.

It wasn't. Lucy had her own ring tone. "It's Lucy. I can't text and drive." Plus, I didn't feel comfortable with Solis digging past the tampon in my purse. On the other hand, if it had been Wilky in the front seat, I would have made him buy me a box. Thinking of that made me mentally chuckle, but it also lowered my mood.

• • •

It was nightfall when we reached Loon Lake. We had just rounded the eastern shore and had started heading west when Solis said to slow down.

"We're coming up on a couple of the locations."

"You're telling me bodies were dumped on the side of the road?"

"No, it's inland, but I'm betting there's a small dirt road that will take us into the woods. I'm sure they didn't hike in."

A few moments later Solis pointed ahead. "There. You see the opening?"

"I see it." I slowed down and made a right onto a bumpy two-track. Twenty feet in, we came upon a steel gate. Madero got out and checked the gate. He shook his head as he walked back to the car. "It's locked up good. Should have brought the bolt cutters."

"A couple of the locations are up ahead, maybe fifteen feet and another fifty feet into the forest," Solis said. "I bet both sides of the road are lined with plots."

I exited the car and stretched for a bit. It felt good after the long drive. The climate up north was cooler and drier than the city. I drew a deep breath and my lungs filled with an earthy, woodsy scent. I looked around and saw that we were surrounded by a thick tangle of trees and brush. The two-track was the only swath that cut through them. The full moon up above helped, but it barely penetrated the forest, leaving it dark and uninviting. The small flashlight I kept in my purse wasn't strong enough to lead a hike into the woods, but I pocketed it just in case.

"This road has to lead us somewhere," I said. "The plots will have to wait."

Finding the Carters was a priority. We started walking. About twenty minutes in, Solis held up his arm and motioned for us to move over to the side.

We didn't question and did what he said. We hid in the brush for a few seconds before he waved us up to his position. Solis pointed down the curved road. "There's a cabin up ahead."

I could barely make out the lines of the structure. Solis had an eagle eye.

We hugged the tree line near the side of the road and made our way forward. I couldn't tell if anybody was home. I didn't see any cars parked out front, but we still hadn't rounded the curve in the road.

As we got closer, the trees around us dispersed and revealed a clear view of the wooden cabin. Sixty feet of open land separated the cabin from our position. The building wasn't very big, maybe seven hundred square feet max. It appeared to have a small second story, either a loft or attic. There were no markings or an address or a welcome sign touting "The Carters"—just the glow.

I noticed the Range Rover parked near the rear of the building. "That's their car."

"If they're home, they're being awfully quiet," Solis said.

"Either that, or they're waiting for us."

74

A few anniversaries ago, Preston had purchased his and hers ATN PVS7 night vision goggles. At the time, Katherine didn't see the value in them. Tonight changed all of that.

From inside the cabin, Preston kept watch on the three individuals. He had come to refer to them as the three amigos. The thought of having three to play with excited him and made him eager to get going with their plan. Katherine came down the stairs and stood next to her husband. He looked like a little boy on Christmas morning, eager to open his presents under the tree. It didn't take her long to spot them. *So clever they think they are.*

Preston saw them early on and watched their slow trek toward the cabin. Step by step, they crept along the side of the road, unaware they had a spotlight on them the entire time.

Upstairs in the tiny attic, the boys were asleep, behind a locked door for their safety. They were not part of the plan. Katherine couldn't risk it. They had already done a wonderful job earlier—distracting the police officer. She had no choice then. That was a worst-case scenario, but she had dutifully planned for it. Just like she had for the scenario they were currently facing. Katherine was a bit surprised when only the three showed up; she had expected more manpower.

She double-checked both guns, making sure the magazines were fully loaded. The two SIG Sauer 228s outfitted with laser sights were a gift from Katherine, spurred by Preston's purchases. He'd reacted to these gifts the same way she had to his—what's the point? He loved his scalpel; it had served him well for so long. Why a gun? He was deadlier his way.

But Katherine said it was all part of the plan. So he learned how to fire it, how to load it, even how to clean it. They did it together; it was often their date night.

Dressed in black from head to toe, guns strapped to their thighs, goggles on top of their heads—they were ready. Preston gave his beautiful wife a loving kiss. When they broke apart, he decided he wanted another, but she stopped him. "There will be plenty of time to play after we're finished."

The plan was to exit through the back of the cabin and head straight to the cover of the trees. From there they would split and circle around the house and flank the three amigos who were still occupying the same spot out front, figuring out a plan of their own—one Katherine thought would be pathetic at best. Before they stepped outside, Katherine turned a small lamp on inside the cabin.

At the tree line, the couple said their goodbyes and

lowered their goggles. If at all possible, they agreed to try to keep the agent alive. She would make a wonderful play toy for Preston, and Katherine simply didn't like the bitch. The thought of being able to watch Kane suffer at the hands of her husband made her smile.

75

"Look, a light came on. They're inside," Solis said while pointing.

"We need to split up," I said. "Solis, you go right. Madero, you go left. There's got to be a back entrance into this place."

"What about you?" Solis asked.

"I'll head for the front door. I'm the shortest; it'll be harder to spot me when I move. It's the only way to take them by surprise."

"One more thing," Solis said. "If the doors are locked, we'll have to fire a round at the knob and kick our way in. We don't have radios so we'll text each other. When we're all in place, we'll push in at once."

As we were about to move, Madero motioned us to stop. "What about the kids?"

Solis looked at the cabin and then back at us. "If they get in my way, they get in my way."

Madero looked at me, obviously wanting to see how I felt about having to target the boys. I didn't think we could trust the children. "Let's not take any chances."

I spotted a wheelbarrow about half the distance between where I crouched and the house. That would be my first destination. I moved as fast as I could, while remaining low, until my back was up against it. Once there, I did a sweep of the property. I could no longer see Solis or Madero. They had disappeared into the darkness. I, on the other hand, felt completely exposed under the moonlight, but I knew better than to think that. The wheelbarrow and I were the same height.

I felt buzzing in my pants. Did they reach the backdoor already? I pulled out my phone, expecting a text from either Solis or Madero, but instead I got one from Lucy. The agent in me screamed, *"What the hell are you doing, Abby?"* as the mother in me texted Lucy back that I was busy. I would have stayed put either way; I hadn't figured out my next move.

I peeked over the wheelbarrow and figured out a plan. I would move straight ahead, up the three stairs, and onto the porch, where I could tuck under a window next to the front door.

On the count of three I would make my move. *One, two*—Bam!

A gunshot!

76

The gunshot came from the right side of the house. *Solis!* No sooner had I heard that one, when I heard another from the left side. *Shit!* They were waiting for us. I heard more firing on the left side but nothing on the right. If I stayed put, I was an easy target on the porch. I reached for the knob. It was locked. I fired a round at the base of the knob. There was more damage than I'd expected, eliminating the need to kick the door open.

I entered the cabin, gun ahead of me. Left. Right. Left. I swung my arms, clearing the area. My finger gripped the trigger tightly. I was so sure one of them would jump out at any minute. I closed the door behind me and crouched down.

The cabin seemed empty. To the left, I saw a small table with a kitchen behind it. To the right of me: a couch, a sitting chair, and a short bookshelf filled with a few knickknacks and paperbacks. Straight ahead were wooden stairs that led up to the second level. *A bedroom. The boys are probably in there.* The door at the top was closed. A tiny office was tucked under the stairs. Next to it was a back door. That's how they got outside.

More shots rang out. *Dammit!* I had no idea what was

going on outside. I bounded up the stairs and plopped myself down on the last step. It was my best bet for cover. From the top of the stairs looking down, I had the front door covered. It would be crazy for me to move outside. I had to trust that Solis and Madero could handle themselves.

I leaned back against the door. Sweat trickled down my face, and my shirt clung to me like a layer of skin. I needed to calm myself and slow my breathing. I turned my head to the side and listened. I couldn't hear any noise or movement coming from the room. Either the boys were being very quiet or they were asleep. My gut told me they were up. The gunshots were loud. I reached up to the knob. Another locked door.

Seconds seemed like minutes. The gunshots outside had died down. I had no idea if Solis or Madero were alive. If they weren't, that would mean the wolves were circling.

77

It didn't take long before Katherine spotted her target moving like a bear on its hind legs. The night-vision goggles painted him as a white human shape against a green background. She wasn't exactly sure which of the two detectives she had been dealt, but she widened her stance and cleared a few branches away. With her breathing slowed and her heartbeat calmed, Katherine was ready.

One, she inhaled. Two, she let it out. Three, she raised her weapon and pulled the trigger.

Through her goggles, she saw the head of the white figure snap back. White particles blasted out from the roundish shape before the figure slumped down into a pile. Bullseye!

• • •

Preston had also spotted his target. He got the taller, fatter one. *This is too easy, fat man. Where's the challenge? Where's the fun? I might as well be aiming a cannon, you pathetic excuse for the living.*

Preston thought of picking him off little by little. Wounding him in each limb, then moving in for a personal kill—the way he loved to do it. That meant going against his wife's wishes of course, something he almost always avoided. She laid out the plan and told Preston not to deviate from it.

Preston bit his lip. He raised his weapon and concentrated. He heard a gunshot just as he pulled his trigger. The rotten timing caused his arm to jerk, sending the double tap he had practiced relentlessly to go wide. He didn't bother with the third shot. He needed to focus. The fat one had already taken advantage of the situation and slipped behind a tree. His belly stuck out of course.

• • •

Madero couldn't see a goddamn thing, but he certainly heard the zip of two bullets fly by him. He knew he wasn't safe behind the tree. The gunman was probably using thermal sighting; it's the only way he could have come that close to hitting him. Madero wasn't even moving when he heard the first shot. But it surprised him enough to jerk back. Had he not, he would have been dead.

The muzzle blasts gave Madero a general location of where the shooter might be. He wasted no time aiming his weapon and pulled the trigger on his department-issued Smith & Wesson. Madero put all fifteen rounds into the area where he believed the shooter's chest and head were. He prayed he had gotten lucky and snagged a headshot.

As quickly as he emptied the magazine, he released it from the gun, pocketed it, and replaced it with a fully loaded one. He was locked and loaded in seconds. These bullets had to count. It was all he had left. He dropped low, hoping he had enough brush covering him. But he knew he couldn't stay still, not if the shooter was still alive. One more thing worried Madero: the gunshot he heard on the other side of the cabin. The Carters were out hunting.

78

Katherine didn't have time to think the situation through thoroughly. She reacted and ran straight for the side of the house when she heard the barrage of return fire that followed what she was sure to be Preston's double tap. *He missed.* She crouched beneath the window on the right side of the cabin, her back pressed up hard against the wood as she caught her breath. Her eyes completed multiple sweeps of the area but nobody came into view. She struggled to quiet herself. She was convinced her labored breaths and thumping heart would give her location away.

She inched forward to the front of the house and peeked around onto the porch. Still her night vision revealed no one. *Where were they? Had the cabin been compromised?* She fell back to the window. Tremors ran through her hands and her rasping breath had become uneven and more pronounced. *Stay calm. Focus.*

She had heard nothing since the last barrage of gunfire. She struggled to keep her thoughts focused; she had no idea if Preston was dead or alive. It terrified her to think she might be by herself. But more importantly, she worried about the boys. Were they still safe?

In the span of a few minutes, the strong matriarch of

the family had gone from confident leader to terrified mother. She couldn't stop thinking about her two boys. Suddenly, images of Jackson and Lorenzo lying dead in a pool of blood filled her head. *No!* She jerked her head. Tears poured down her cheeks. Her bottom lip quivered uncontrollably. Katherine crumpled to the ground. *I can't lose the boys. I can't! What if I gave up? I could say Preston made me a prisoner and forced me. Would they believe me?* That maternal instinct kicked in. All Katherine could think about was protecting her kids, even if that meant giving herself up.

She flipped the night vision goggles up and brushed her hair from her face. Slowly, she raised herself up until her eyes could see through the dusty window. Her vision was slightly obstructed, and she needed to be sure if someone was inside or not. She pulled down on the sleeve of her sweater so it covered her palm and wiped a very tiny portion of the lower corner of the window so she could peek through again. She saw nothing.

• • •

I hid easily in the darkness at the top of the stairs with my black jeans and blue long-sleeve shirt. It's the only reason why I could look directly at Katherine while her eyes glazed over my position. I had initially heard someone bump up against the side of the house. A few seconds later, I had seen her head pop up for just split second, but I instantly recognized the headgear she had on. *Night-vision goggles*. Solis and Madero were easy targets. They never had a chance against the couple.

And now the dynamic duo had me in their sights.

Katherine peeked inside once more, sans goggles, and then disappeared, but it was easy to track her. I heard her step up onto the porch. If she hadn't noticed the missing lock, she would any second now. Until then, she probably thought the house had not been breached. I knew she wanted into the bedroom where her children were. That's where she would make her stand. Not knowing the situation outside, I had to assume the worst: Solis and Madero were down and the wolves were coming into the den.

I couldn't wait any longer. I took a chance Katherine was in front of the door. I lifted my weapon and unloaded my entire magazine, starting near the bottom of the door, shooting up methodically—hoping I would hit her.

• • •

Madero knew his next move had to be to a place providing better coverage. He was an open target in the woods and no match against a pair of night vision-wearing lunatics. If he could get to the space between the SUV and the house, he would have the protection he needed. Whoever had shot at him would have no choice but to come out into the open.

Madero gave himself the best starting block takeoff he could manage. He ran hard and straight. Not once did he look around at his surrounding area. The way Madero saw it, if he got hit, he got hit.

As soon as he exited the tree line, he heard rapid gunfire. Madero ducked his head and kept running, all while wondering how many times he had been shot. He slid into the gap between the house and the vehicle like a ballplayer. Looking back and forth between the front and back of the vehicle, he waited for his attacker to show but no one came. He lowered his gun and patted himself, checking for wounds. *What the...?* He thought for sure he had taken a slug.

With no movement in the woods, Madero figured he had hit his target, or at least wounded it. *What about the other gunfire? Who were they shooting at? Solis? Kane?* For some reason, his gut told him the husband had hunted him. Madero pulled out his cell and sent a text to Kane and Solis, wondering who was still alive.

79

My phone buzzed against my leg, causing my body to jerk. I reached into my jean pocket and pulled out my cell. Madero was alive. I quickly answered him. "I'm okay. In the house. You? Solis?"

Madero buzzed me a second later. "I'm okay. Between Rover and house. Solis MIA."

"There's a door, back of house. I'm at top of stairs," I texted.

Madero responded, "I'm coming in."

Seconds later I heard the door open and close. "Madero," I whispered.

"I'm inside," he said. I watched Madero move into view at the bottom of the stairs.

"Katherine was in front of the door. I think I hit her."

"No shit," he said looking at all the bullet holes. Madero continued forward until he had his back up against the wall near the hinged part of the front door. I moved so he could see me on the stairs. He nodded and I motioned to him to pull the door open. I aimed the barrel of my gun straight ahead.

Madero reached across the door, slipped his fingers into a bullet hole, and pulled. The door swung open as he moved to the side and raised his weapon in case a madman or woman came running in. No one did.

Katherine lay curled up on the porch. Madero moved toward the doorway.

"Is she dead?" I asked.

Madero leaned over for a closer look. He then fired off a round. "If she wasn't, she is now," he said turning around with a spiteful look.

I couldn't believe what I had witnessed. *Did Madero just murder Katherine, or was she already dead?* Did I even care?

Madero continued to look my way, waiting for an answer to what he just did. What he got instead, neither of us saw coming.

An arm reached around Madero's neck and pulled back, twisting his head off to the side. When he turned back toward me, his eyes widened in disbelief. Blood gushed down his throat as he cupped his neck with his right hand.

What was happening? He shot her. I saw it myself.

Madero dropped to his knees, his stare never leaving mine as he gasped for air. I shook my head. It couldn't be. No!

Grinning from cheek to cheek behind Madero stood a tall, bloodied man with his tousled mane matted to the sides of his face. I knew that hair, no mistaking it; Preston Carter was alive.

Quicker than I could ever have imagined, he moved

from the door to the bottom of the stairs and bounded up, two at a time. I raised my weapon. Preston closed in on me—only four steps away. His arm swung upward. The scalpel still gripped tightly. My weapon had yet to finish its upward swing. He was too close. I needed more room and pressed up further against the door. I had time for one shot. *Make it count, Abby.*

80

His head snapped back as skull and brain erupted from behind it. Tilting back on his heels, Preston Carter fell. Smoke rose from the dark hole at the center of his forehead. His blue eyes were already lifeless. The fall seemed to last an eternity. When he hit the floor, he lay sprawled on his back with a blank stare. His head tilted to the side as blood pooled underneath.

I let out a large breath of air, not realizing I had been holding it. My eyes were transfixed on Preston's lifeless body, as if I somehow expected him to rise up and come after me again. Was he dead? Should I incorporate the Madero Method? I looked at the slumped-over detective. He was still alive before Preston made his move toward me, but now he lay motionless. *They were all dead,* I thought, until I heard a noise behind the door. A soft crying, barely audible.

I pressed the left side of my face against the cool wood, so my lips were where the door met the frame.

"Lorenzo? Jackson? Can you hear me? It's Agent Kane… everything is okay. No one is going to hurt you… you're safe now. Please unlock the door."

I listened for movement and heard rustling, followed by squeaks in the floorboards. The knob jiggled, and then I heard a click. Slowly the door opened, revealing a little boy with puffy, red eyes. I quickly entered the darkened room and shut the door behind me. "You must be Jackson," I said.

He nodded his head before jumping into my arms. "Everything is fine," I whispered, my eyes searching for his brother. He sat quietly in the corner, sniffling. I reached out with my arm. "Come, Lorenzo. You're safe. I won't hurt you."

81

It was a long night at the cabin.

I stayed in the room with the boys until the first unit arrived. There were three mattresses laid across the floor, taking up the width. The space was obviously a makeshift bedroom, and long stays, if any, were not the norm. The boys continued to ask about their parents, especially the little one, Jackson.

"Mommy and Daddy are very sick. They have to see a doctor." I didn't want to lie, but what else could I tell them?

"Are they going to be okay?" Jackson asked.

"Let's hope so." I gave him a hug.

I felt terrible for the two. They were young and innocent. Clearly they loved their mother and had only done what she had asked them to. I didn't blame them. In fact, it angered me that she had taken advantage of them. It reminded me of those parents who used their kids to distract salespeople so they could shoplift. What a despicable act.

When I first entered the attic space, I noticed an earbud from an MP3 player in Jackson's ear. The other one dangled in front of his chest; it's probably why he heard me and opened the door. A tiny window allowed a few rays of moonlight into the room, but my eyes still needed time to adjust.

I fetched my mini flashlight from my pocket and surveyed the boys and the rest of the room. They were both dressed in jeans, sweaters, and Tigers baseball caps. Each had their own backpack filled with a change of clothes and a few toys and books. Lorenzo also had an MP3 player and used it while sitting contently in the corner.

I spotted a mini cooler against the wall. Inside were juice containers, a couple of yogurts, and a plastic dish with chopped fruit inside. Jackson crawled over.

"Would you like something to eat?" I asked.

He nodded and pointed to a container filled with fruit. Before popping a grape into his mouth, he smiled at me, the first and only smile I would see all night. Obviously thought had gone into keeping the boys comfortable—though I suspected the real purpose of the MP3 players was to shield them from hearing what was likely to happen outside the room.

As the night wore on, Jackson succumbed to sleep while his head lay in my lap. I ran my fingers through his hair and couldn't help but wonder about what effects all that had happened would have on them. Were they damaged goods? Would they remember anything? Worse yet, would they turn out like their parents? Did either of the two inherit the genetic makeup for violent behavior?

My eyes welled as these sad thoughts flowed through my head. I couldn't imagine my kids having to endure such an ordeal. It made me miss Ryan and Lucy even more. Interestingly enough, I couldn't help but compare myself to Katherine. Even with all she and Preston were facing, that woman still had the mindset to ensure the boys were comfortable and taken care of. Part of me had expected the boys to be half-dressed, hungry, and in need of a bath. It was quite the opposite. *Was she a better mother to her kids than I was to mine?*

I quickly shook that thought out of my head. It was ridiculous to even think that. Katherine was nothing more than a cold-blooded killer, right?

I called out more than once for Lorenzo to join us, but he wouldn't budge, which was fine by me. In all honesty, I couldn't quite tell if he knew what had taken place outside that door. Was the young boy smart enough to know what his parents had planned, or worse, what they were? I was pretty sure in little Jackson's eyes, Katherine was simply Mom.

When I heard the approach of the first siren, I told both boys, "Lock the door and don't open it for anybody but me." I wanted to get them out of there as soon as possible, but I also didn't want them to see what had happened to their parents.

It took time, but we were able to remove the boys an hour later when Child Protective Services arrived. The bodies were still strewn about the cabin floor, so we did our best to cover them before I escorted the two boys out.

A few officers found Solis' body off to the right side of the house. He had suffered a fatal gunshot to the head. Preston Carter had been shot multiple times, but they were all superficial wounds, hence the reason for his reprieve. I'd gotten lucky with Katherine and had hit her three times in the chest. From the look of the wounds, it should have killed her, but I couldn't be sure. I knew her autopsy would reveal that the head wound came from Madero's gun. Maybe she did move. Maybe she did reach for her gun. Sitting at the top of the stairs, I couldn't see her. Madero's wide stance had blocked my view.

When Lieutenant White arrived, he made it his business to find me right away. One look at his body movement told me he wasn't happy about the situation. I thought he would be, considering we had caught the killers.

"I told you guys to stay put. I know you got my message, so don't say you didn't."

"Had we waited and mobilized with a tactical unit, we would have run the risk of the Carters disappearing for good."

"You don't know that!"

"You keep telling me what I know. Guess what? I know I caught the killers," I said, folding my arms across my chest. It didn't matter what White had to say; I was determined to stand my ground—even when he delivered a cheap blow.

"And got Solis and Madero killed."

Insinuating their deaths were the result of my judgment call was beyond bullshit. I took a deep breath in hopes it would help to calm my nerves. I was a popcorn kernel of a degree away from exploding. "Look, Lieutenant, we all knew the risk." My voice was steadier than I had anticipated. "No one was forced to do anything here. So don't you dare accuse me of endangering your men."

"All I'm doing is pointing—"

"Don't interrupt me. I have the floor, and you will show me a little respect and hear what I have to say. Is that understood?" I knew White was a ranking officer with Detroit police but he wasn't my boss. And anyway, it went beyond protocol; it was about common courtesy. White gritted his teeth and pursed his lips before acknowledging me with a nod.

"We couldn't risk waiting," I continued. "They were heading back underground."

"Why would you think that? There are six RRs. There's still one left."

"Not true. According to Ellen Scott, there were five, not six. Elliot Hardin made a mistake."

"What makes you so quick to believe her over Hardin?"

I shrugged. "She was adamant about it. My guess is, they were more afraid of what would happen if they came out than they were of the Carters. And as you can see," I said, looking around us, "the Carters went on the run."

White let out a deep breath and rubbed his hand back and forth over his bald head. "That doesn't mean there aren't six RRs," he mumbled as he turned away to look at the property. "We lost two good men today," he said, still facing away from me.

"Don't you think I know that?" I shook my head and shifted my weight to my other leg. I looked around at the manpower surrounding me, the people dusting, bagging, and photographing, even the ones moving the bodies. They were all here to help to bring the case to a close. *You did well, Agent.* That was the phrase that should accompany my internal pat on the back.

I'm guessing from the way White's shoulders dropped, he accepted the reality of what had happened. He further deflated by letting out a heavy breath and lowering his head. His eyes eventually found their way back to me. "Agent Kane, you did good. You got our killers in the end."

I nodded in agreement.

"Don't think I'm against you here. I do appreciate everything you've done."

I let my gaze roam the scene around us. It had started to grow chaotic. Different departments of law enforcement had descended onto the property. I didn't even want to think about the manpower needed for the forensics investigation of all those burial plots. Unimaginable. But it was over. That's what mattered.

Still, there was one bit that bothered me—the cover-up.

"Lieutenant," I said, "I found a book at the Carter's residence. It's what led us here." I filled him in on the details.

"So you're saying from the Garrison arrest forward, they hunted various street people and then buried all of those victims here?"

I nodded. "Well, we're assuming their victims were street people. No one to report their disappearance. We'll know for sure once they start uncovering the bodies."

I watched him bounce the thought around for a bit. He seemed to buy the theory. "Why bury them and not the RRs?" he asked. "What's the reason for making them public?"

"Katherine wanted revenge. She wanted to instill fear in the executives, let them know someone was after them."

White nodded. "She's been married to that psycho for some time. I wonder why she waited until now."

"Maybe she didn't know enough about them and needed time to track them down," I offered.

"Sheesh, those two were a perfect match for each other. What are the odds?" White grabbed hold of his pants and tugged them up.

"You know, your 24/7 surveillance team should have picked up on this place."

White's eye's narrowed in on me. "What are you getting at, Agent?"

"If that team had done their job, this place should have

sounded the alarm."

"You're right." The Lieutenant held up the notebook in his hands. "Maybe it would have led us to the Carters or this book sooner. For now, I'll hang on to it." He then shoved the notebook into his back pocket.

I opened my mouth to speak but stopped myself. White must have sensed what I was going to say.

"Let it be. It doesn't matter now. It's over. You can go home, and I can go back to counting the days to retirement." White held his pleading stare until someone called out for him. Before walking away, he repeated what he had told me once already. "It's bigger than you and me."

82

The drive back to Detroit was long and arduous—lonesome, too, if I were to be honest. I missed sitting in the passenger seat while Wilkinson watched me fix my lipstick from the corner of his eye. I still had trouble believing he was gone. The mornings at the hotel were sad reminders. There were times I expected to see him in the lobby waiting with a coffee for him and a green tea for me. I wished he were.

There were a lot of things I wished I had done differently—like not playing hard to get for as long as I did, or saying yes to more of those late-night drinks. I wished I had taken him seriously sooner.

Since the murder of my husband, my social life had been scarce, like the ice age. I had almost forgotten what sex was like until that night with Wilkinson. Even though I hurt between my legs the next day, I had been ready for round two.

It's not like I didn't want to date after Peng's death. There were plenty of opportunities, but it had felt like I would have been cheating on him. Wilkinson broke through, though. He helped me open myself up again. And now he was gone, too.

Since his death, I'd spent more time than I wanted lying awake in bed, thinking about what I could have done differently that night. There were a million ways we could have approached the situation. Would the outcome have changed? Perhaps. I try not to beat myself up about it. I could run multiple scenarios through my head that would lead to a positive outcome, but it wouldn't be fair. With hindsight, one can always skew the results.

The truth was, the case was screwy from the start. The more I thought about the cover-up, the angrier I became, even though it had no direct effect on Wilkinson's death. I wanted it to. It would be something I could blame.

I couldn't shake it. How does a cover-up that big go unnoticed? A corrupt city, that's how. Wild scenarios swam around inside my head. None of it made any sense. My imagination started to get the best of me.

Honestly, part of me didn't want to know what had really happened. Finding out could result in career death. White was right; people much more powerful than the chiefs were involved.

• • •

I decided to stick around for a few more days to finish up my report at the central precinct. It wasn't necessary to be in Detroit to finish; the only reason would be if I wanted to continue investigating the cover-up.

I still had access to the necessary case files and spent most of the day combing through them again, trying to glean anything I could, when I heard a knock on the office door. I looked up to find Reginald Reed standing there. "Chief Reed."

He motioned for me to remain seated. "Don't get up. I'm glad you're still here. I wanted to personally thank you for all your help, Agent."

"I wish I could echo your enthusiasm, but the loss of three good men dampens my spirits a bit."

"I understand," he said, pausing awkwardly. "I bet you're eager to get back to your family."

"I am, but I thought I'd wrap up my report here, while everything was still fresh in my head."

Reed looked around the room. A few of the boxes were open, and case files lay strewn about my desk. One didn't need to be a top-notch detective to see I wasn't writing up my report.

"You're being thorough with your report, I take it?"

Did he ask me a trick question? Reed had to know I didn't need to plow through the case files for my report, at least not to the extent it appeared. I decided to play along with the top guy. "I am."

"Good to hear. It's important the facts are kept straight. I keep all my facts tucked away in my desk, left bottom drawer, in a manila folder marked 'miscellaneous'." Reed eyed me for a moment before turning around and leaving.

He couldn't have been any clearer.

I hung around the precinct later than I had planned, late

enough for the day shift to clock out, and more specifically, for Reed's administrative assistant to leave. I had already done a walk-by past his office earlier, but the timing wasn't right. There were too many uniforms milling around. Getting caught snooping in the big man's sanctuary wasn't something I wanted to explain to my superiors.

To kill time, I called Po Po to see how things were going and to let her know I would be home in a couple of days. Our conversation was short, a struggle really to get beyond one-word answers. Luckily, Ryan and Lucy had come home from school, so I got to hear all about Lucy's day.

"I painted a big dog and he was blue, and then I painted a flower and it was blue, and then I painted a sun and it was blue, and then I painted a caterpillar and he was blue…"

By my count, Lucy had painted a total of ten blue things at school. She went on to tell me about snack time; they had orange slices. My heart fell out of my chest as I listened to her. I could have been home now, walking her back from school and hearing about her day firsthand. But no, I had made the decision to pursue a case that, by all accounts, didn't really matter anymore.

When I got off the phone, I headed straight to Reed's office.

The coast looked clear. I reached for the knob. For a split second, doubt skipped around inside my head. Had I understood my conversation with the chief correctly? When the knob turned and I closed the door behind me, I knew I had heard exactly what he wanted me to hear.

I took a moment to survey the room before moving over to the desk. *Left bottom drawer.* I grabbed the handle, and even though I saw a lock on it, I knew it would be open.

Inside were a few hanging files. Lying on the bottom, I saw a manila folder labeled, "Misc." Inside, I found a small leather-bound book. It was a diary. After flipping through a few pages, I realized Reed had kept a detailed account of all the monthly meetings he had with the mayor of Detroit, Leon Briggs.

83

I spent the next two hours holed up in Reed's office reading everything he had written in the diary. Most of the questions I had about Garrison and his case were answered right here. Reed was very particular in his note taking. It was as if he knew one day someone would need to know what had happened.

It didn't take long for me to realize the mayor really did run that city. Turns out very few people were allowed access to the information on Garrison's case, but it didn't stop Reed from writing it all down.

On numerous occasions, he pointed out the fact that no real evidence tied Garrison to the murders before the Comerica robbery. Reed knew, and so did the other chiefs at the table I had met when I first arrived. Even White knew. But they all ended up following the orders of the mayor. That's a lot of brass putting their butts on the line for one man. What was it about Mayor Briggs that had these men caving to these insane requests?

The discovery didn't stop there. Further reading revealed the attorney general, the prosecutor for the city, and the defense for Garrison knew about the lack of evidence. Their job was to make sure the holes were closed.

It was unbelievable. I felt like I was trapped inside a wild crime novel. Never in a million years would I have suspected something like that could actually happen in real life. Movies? Sure. In the city of Detroit? Apparently.

It was getting late. I figured his office and desk would not be accessible the next day, or any day after for that matter, so I made sure I had all the information I needed. I took notes and snapped pictures but stopped short of taking anything. If I were to actually tackle the job of revealing the cover-up, common sense would say I would need his notes as evidence. That's when I realized I was still unsure whether I wanted to create problems for myself. I followed my instincts and left the office.

I reached my hotel a little after nine. I had "Hot Bath" flashing like a neon sign in my head. I hoped it would help me think through the dilemma that had decided to toy with me.

I immediately got a bath going and removed my clothes. It felt good to feel the cool air against my skin. The humidity was one thing I would not miss. While I waited for the tub to fill, I poured myself a hefty serving of Jameson, neat. I let the first sip roll around my tongue for a bit—such a familiar and delicious taste. After a few swirls, I let it slip down my throat and warm my chest. That was the liquor's way of telling me everything would work out. It always did.

It took a few more sips and a couple more swirls before the tub was filled. I eased myself into the warm waters until

I felt my butt touch bottom. Nothing beats a bath. My favorite thing to do was point my toes forward and stretch my legs, triggering a full body quiver. I always followed that up with a yawn.

After a few minutes, I started considering my options—to pursue or not to pursue. That was the obvious elephant in the room. Even if I did decide to move forward, it didn't mean I had to work it. I could just turn over the evidence and my report to my supervisor. Or I could push ahead like I normally would and deal with the fallout.

Now that I was aware of Mayor Briggs' involvement, I had to decide whether to confront him. I didn't feel the need to follow up with Reed at the moment, since he'd already given up the mayor. I suspected Briggs ordered the cover-up. Next up was to find out why.

That seemed to be the only question bouncing around in my head. Why risk so much to frame Garrison? Whatever it was, it had something to do with the mayor. Everyone else appeared to be following his orders; they were too scared not to. There were a lot of powerful people falling in line. They could have stood up to him. How big of a son of a bitch was that guy?

So Briggs convinced everyone to go along with the cover-up. Okay, everyone's crooked. Fine, I'll buy that. Money talks. But how did Briggs know it would work? How did he know the original killer would stop killing so his plan to frame Garrison could work? That's when it hit me.

I jumped out of the tub and called White.

"This is Lieutenant White."

"Lieutenant, it's Agent Kane… he knew."

"What are you talking about, Agent?"

"Briggs. He knew the Carters."

84

That same night, Mayor Briggs was also twirling his thoughts around. He was busy figuring out what to do with Abby Kane.

Stevie and the mayor were tucked away in his office downing glasses of scotch while they did what they did best: schemed. When they heard Agent Kane had caught the killers and they were dead, they celebrated like everyone else. Why not? The big gorilla on their back had just climbed off. Mayor Briggs had waited a long time for that to happen, and he let himself enjoy it. But like most things in Detroit, the party didn't last very long.

Instead of going home, like she should have, Agent Kane chose to stick around and poke her little head where it didn't belong. She was officially more than an irritant.

"How can a person be so smart at one thing and a fool at another?" Briggs asked out loud as he leaned back in his leather chair.

Stevie didn't bother to answer; he knew his boss was just talking. And so long as he talked, the chief of staff listened. Enough time had passed. Stevie decided he had waited long enough and updated Briggs of Agent Kane's situation. They had both thought she'd left Detroit, until

Stevie heard otherwise.

"My sources told me she was at central all day. That's not all, though."

Briggs turned to Stevie with an arch in his eyebrow sharp enough to poke an eye out. "What? Spit it out."

"I heard she spent time in Reed's office tonight."

"He talked?"

"He wasn't there, but I wouldn't put it past Reed to have left something out for her to find. That meticulous motherfucker is a liability. Always was. Should have buried his ass a long time ago."

Briggs shifted his eyes toward Stevie. "You know I needed him to make this happen."

Stevie sat up in his chair. "Nigga ain't worth shit now."

"He needs to be dealt with, but my concern is with the woman. She's too close to the stove. Fuck if I'mma get burned."

"What's the plan, boss?" Stevie asked as he fingered the rim of his glass.

The mayor leaned back into his chair and took a deep breath before letting it out slowly. He was dealing with an FBI agent. She didn't fall under his command or take orders from the head of the local FBI office. It was hard enough getting Special Agent Tully on board, but Briggs knew all those years of giving that man freebie jaunts to Windsor, Canada for nights in the casinos and the high-end brothels would pay off.

That was how Briggs had operated for as long as anyone could remember. He would work to win over anyone who had any cachet until they owed him. There were holdouts, though, Reed being one of them.

Briggs had wanted to appoint Reed to the top position of chief of police for a while. The job would have been the silver lining in a long career in law enforcement, and Reed wanted it—but he didn't want the baggage that came with it.

Of course, the mayor realized if he gave Reed the job, it wouldn't be enough to secure his unwavering loyalty to do his bidding without question. No, no, no. He needed a hook. Reed would need to owe him for a long time. When Mayor Briggs found out about Reed's sick wife, he didn't send flowers. Instead, he wiped out the $250,000 dollar balance at the hospital and then sweetened the pot with a $100,000 credit for future treatments, anonymously of course.

It didn't take Reed long to realize what had happened. He had taken the bait as expected, and now, he was hooked.

Reed stopped fighting and gave in. They all did eventually. Everyone in the city was a friend of the mayor, and they all wished he were dead. Somehow and some way, Briggs had flipped every single one of them, and now he owned them.

Simply put, Mayor Briggs had the city by the balls. And he enjoyed squeezing them.

85

White reluctantly agreed to meet me in the lounge area of my hotel.

"Care to elaborate?" White asked, drink already in hand. I watched him slide into the oversized lounge chair and let out a long breath. The precinct was a ten-minute walk away, yet White acted like he had to climb Mt. Hood to meet me.

I ignored his antics and continued where I had left off earlier. "Briggs had to have known the Carters. It's the only way he could guarantee the Garrison cover-up would work. It makes no sense to bully everyone into going along with his plan if it wouldn't work."

"Whoa, wait a minute here. You're saying Leon Briggs, the mayor of Detroit, was friendly with a couple of serial killers?"

"Put your hands down and cut the dramatics," I told him. "You know damn well what I'm saying."

White's flat expression hung steady on his face. I had come on strong, but I was tired of dancing around the bush. He needed to stop hindering the investigation and just get on board. "It makes sense," I said, raising my glass at him. "You know it does."

White remained silent. He looked dumbstruck. Apparently, I had rung the truth bell.

"Did you know?" I asked.

White licked his lips.

"Do you honestly believe Briggs would pal around with a pair of murdering psychopaths?"

I didn't bother to answer him. I didn't feel the need to repeat myself.

White rubbed his hands together. His face grew tight. "Let me tell you a little about our mayor. He has got a grip on this city like no other."

"What do you mean? He tells everyone what to do?"

"That's a pretty good way to put it. I already know your next question, so I'll go ahead and answer it. The few that challenged him…" White shook his head, "they just up and disappeared. Ain't been seen for years."

"So if you're not with the mayor, you're against him."

White nodded. "We all learned not to question. People accepted the situation they were in, and when asked to do something, they did it. After Garrison was put away, the murders stopped. Whatever questions we had went away. Those who might have known, the surveillance team, they're dead. Whatever answers they had to your questions they took to their graves."

"You just admitted that Garrison was framed."

White smiled and finished the last of his drink.

"So it's also possible the surveillance team knew more

than what you or others were led to believe?"

White nodded as he crunched on an ice cube.

"Well, that explains why you didn't know about the property up north."

"Exactly. We didn't even know the hostages' names. That's how secretive it was."

We both sat quietly in our chairs, lost in our thoughts about the discussion we were having. Accusing the mayor of having the Carters on his payroll was crazy. Who on earth would believe us? But it made sense. He had to have some relationship or connection with them. For the Carters to stop all public kills for five years at the time they were trying to frame Garrison was too perfect. But then it clicked for me.

"That's it." I sat up straight.

"What?" White asked.

"If the surveillance team did discover the truth about the surviving hostages—the Carters—Briggs could have struck a deal with them. We in law enforcement strike deals with criminals all the time in exchange for testimony. It's called the Witness Protection Program. And they all go into hiding."

"You're saying he put them in the program?"

"I know he's a powerful man, but he's not that powerful. The mayor put them into his own personal protection program, one that still allowed them to keep on killing, with conditions of course."

White held up his hand and counted off. "No public kills. Concentrate on street people. Bury the bodies. Sounds like a great deal to me. But what does Briggs get in return?"

"Their services," I said.

86

I was beat. The conversation with White, the drinks, it all took its toll on me and sent me straight to dreamland as soon as I returned to my room. I wasn't sure how long I had been out, but I remembered stirring just a tiny bit when I had rolled over until I lay half on my side, half on my stomach—the best position. And I would have been out in a few seconds if it weren't for that metal clicking noise I swore I had heard.

It sounded as if someone had just entered my room. My back faced the door, and I had no idea if that person had a weapon or not. Advantage: intruder.

I heard the faint movement of a shoe brush across the carpet. My skin tingled, sounding the alarm. I had to hurry. I needed to put the bed between the intruder and me. I remembered my weapon being holstered and hanging off the desk chair next to the window side of the bed. I could slide across the sheets, hit the floor, grab my weapon, and throw the drapes open, letting the moonlight shine inside. Advantage: me.

Everything works in theory.

I had wasted enough time. I threw off the blanket cover and kicked my legs out. Reaching with my right arm, I grabbed a fistful of sheet and pulled myself over. My legs weren't long enough to do it all in one movement. I kicked again, and that time I felt the edge of the bed. Just as I sat up and my legs were sliding off the bed, a crushing weight came down, pinning me on my side.

My attacker was male, no surprise. I couldn't recognize him since my face was buried in the pillow. He was heavy, obviously much taller than I. I tried to kick him off, but it was like moving a large block of cement that had fallen on me. I needed to conserve my energy. I had lost whatever advantage I may have had.

His breathing was labored, and he smelled of alcohol. I hoped that was the advantage coming back my way. Wrong. In one movement, he flipped me on to my back and slipped between my naked legs, forcing me open. *Is he going to rape me?*

I struggled to no avail. *This can't be happening.* And yet it was. I prepared myself mentally for what might come. My hair still obstructed my view, keeping my attacker faceless. I shook my head back and forth in an effort to clear it. That's when he first spoke.

"You're a feisty bitch, ain't you?" he said.

That voice. I've heard it before. Where?

Before I could identify him, he started kissing my neck while he mumbled about how he hadn't had a woman like me. It disgusted me. He gripped both of my wrists and had my arms stretched above my head. He maneuvered a little so he could pin one of my arms down with his forearm while he grabbed the other. It freed up his other hand. Within seconds, he had unzipped his pants and freed himself. I could feel him pressed up against the outside of my vagina, and it made my skin tighten. I felt nauseated as he moved against me. Reality had set in. It was going to happen.

"Please," I said, "let me at least get a condom." I didn't have any, but I needed to try to create some sort of a diversion. It was my only hope.

That's when he said, "Stevie don't do condoms."

Stevie Roscoe—the mayor's chief of staff.

How? Why? He lifted his head up and looked me in the face. He obviously didn't care that I could recognize him. In fact, he blew the rest of my hair out of my face so I could have a better look. I did. His darkened eyes held their glare on me. He didn't blink; he just stared into me. He had a frozen smile that revealed blocky teeth. I turned away when he started to thrust.

I thought of giving up and letting him get on with it. Maybe it wouldn't take long. But I couldn't do that. I wouldn't let myself do that. I wracked my brain for something to say. I still had time to talk him out of it.

"Why, Stevie? Why are you doing this?"

"Stevie got a big dick. Stevie goin' fill you up real nice."

Hadn't he heard a word I had said? "But you work for

the mayor."

"No shit, Sherlock. But I like fucking hot women." Stevie had to slide down a little to avoid stabbing my stomach with his erection. He spit into his hand and then reached down between my legs. I felt his coarse fingers rub against my folds. I was losing the battle. I could feel him dragging himself across me, searching for my opening. *No, this can't be happening.*

Then he found it.

Any second now.

87

"Get ready, bitch," he said as he looked back up at me, his nose squarely in front of my forehead.

Thank you. Advantage had come back to my side. With all the force I could muster, I threw my forehead straight into Stevie's face, crushing his nose.

Stevie jerked away, screaming. "You fucking bitch."

I wasn't out of the woods yet. He still lay completely on top of me, but he had let go of my arms. I shoved my hand down between us and grasped twice. Nothing. I tried again. That time, I came up with a handful of scrotum. Like a vise grip, my hand clamped on and squeezed as hard as it could.

Stevie roared in pain and did his best to move away from me. I didn't let go of him. I held my grip like my life depended on it. As he rolled over to the side, I rolled on top of him and then off the bed. I reached out for my weapon with my free arm, but it was too far away. I had to let go.

Within seconds, I had my weapon drawn and pointed at Stevie, who continued to roll around on the bed in agony. I reached behind me and threw the curtains open to let the moonlight into the room. Stevie sat up at that moment. I couldn't understand a word he said, but he had recovered.

"Don't do it!" I shouted.

His eyes remained locked on me as forceful breaths snarled through his nostrils like an enraged bull.

"Stevie…" I warned.

He didn't listen. Off the bed he shot, barreling toward me with both arms out. At the academy, they taught us to "shoot to stop" and to shoot "center mass." I raised my weapon. *Not this time.*

The bullet struck Stevie in the head and threw him back onto the bed. I thought of putting two more slugs into him as I moved over to the desk to turn the lamp on. But the damage I had inflicted was clearer now. He had a small crater between his eyes.

• • •

I made my first call to the front desk. I wanted a new room, *pronto*. Then I called 911. A few minutes passed before the units arrived. I told them to secure the area; I would be back.

My new room for the night was a couple floors down on the other side of the building. I had a river view. I sat on the bed for a bit, contemplating my situation. I had come close to being raped and most likely killed. I thought about Po Po and the kids. What was the contingency plan if something were to happen to me? I didn't know. What kind of terrible mother doesn't have that thought out? Me. That's who.

My ego had to understand that it was no longer about

the life and times of Abby Kane. I was the parent of two small children and the caretaker of an elderly woman who, in fact, did a whole lot of caretaking back at home. Life didn't need to revolve around fighting crime. It was about them, too. I wrote down a reminder to increase my life insurance when I returned to San Francisco.

The other nagging bit bothering me was a sense of loneliness. I didn't feel like I had anybody watching my back. My partner was gone. So were the only detectives I trusted. I had no support out here.

The uniforms in the other room could be part of the cover-up. Everyone I trusted was dead. Even my supervisor had no idea what was going on. Part of me said, "Go home. Get the hell out of there." The other part said, "Nail the bastards." I knew I had outlived my welcome. I didn't care though.

Stevie Roscoe had been sent to kill me that night. That bastard figured he could get a little action beforehand. Now he was dead and his balls were mush.

• • •

When I returned to the crime scene on the fourteenth floor, CSI had just arrived. I was half a step behind them as we made our way through the hallway. A few nosy guests peeked from their rooms, wondering what had happened. In another doorway, a woman dressed only in a frilly thong and a matching bra flashed a flirtatious smile.

"What happened?" she asked the gentlemen in front of

me.

"Rapist. Still loose," I answered without missing a beat. *The next time you want some attention, try something else.*

Upon entering the room, I noticed a pair of suits talking quietly in the far corner of the room, near the body. *Detectives?* They didn't look familiar. *Trust no one, Abby.*

88

It didn't take long for the crime-fighting duo to make their way over to me. They were white males dressed in dark blue suits. They looked young—recently promoted most likely, considering the call came in at two in the morning. Neither of them cracked a smile or showed any warmth. My conversation with them would be all business, fine. *Trust no one, Abby.*

"Agent Kane?" The taller one asked as he took out a notepad.

"That's me."

"Sorry about what happened to you tonight." He motioned with his head.

I acknowledged his attempt at compassion.

"I'm Detective Rolland Russo. This is my partner, Detective Denny Hopper."

Hopper stuck his hand out for a quick shake. Russo continued with his cold approach. I told them everything that had happened and answered their questions. Russo asked not a single question more than needed to conduct a capable investigation. I knew where it was headed: nowhere. I would be folded into the cover-up. Everyone here played for the same team. Felt like serious *Stepford*

Wives stuff.

"If we're done, I'd like to head over to the hospital so I can have a rape kit administered."

The iceman looked up from his notepad. "You think that's necessary?"

"Why would you ask that?"

"Well, according to your answers, you weren't really raped," he said looking down at his notes. "Plus, there's a body. So…?"

I couldn't believe that jackass. *What kind of cop tries to deter a victim of a sexual assault from completing a rape kit? I bet things would be different if iceman here had some guy trying to poke his way into his behind.* The guy was thick. He made Madero seem brilliant.

I leaned in. "I'm going to have the hospital administer the rape kit. While they're doing that, I'm going to film it on my phone. And then, I'm going to personally deliver the kit to you," I said holding up the business card he gave me earlier. "If for some reason the evidence goes missing, whether you are involved with it or not, I will open a federal investigation on you for tampering with evidence, and I will make it my lifelong mission to see to it you suffer in ways your small brain couldn't possibly fathom."

Before the ape could answer, I did a one-eighty and walked out of the room. Time was a factor with rape kits. And yes, I knew Stevie Roscoe was dead on the floor, but considering how corrupt that city was, I wanted to make sure everything having to do with my attack didn't conveniently disappear.

89

Two hours later, I made good on my promise by hand-delivering the kit to Detective Russo at the central precinct. I of course filmed myself handing it over and then him checking it into evidence. He was not impressed to say the least. Fine by me; I wasn't trying to be his buddy.

I swung by White's office later on the off chance he would be an early bird, in at 6:30 a.m. No such luck. The door to his office was closed, and the lights were off. My next stop was the office Wilkinson and I had been using. What I found inside triggered a sudden coldness throughout my body.

The room had been completely cleared of all the case files and any trace of Wilkinson and I working here for the last month. It was now a fully functioning office. And it looked as though that person had been in there for years. *What was going on?*

There was a single desk with a leather chair behind it. Heavily stuffed file cabinets lined the walls. A current calendar hung on the wall. There were even family pictures. From what I could gather, the office belonged to an Officer McCormack. The name didn't ring a bell. I knew I was tired, but I certainly wasn't imagining things. It was the right office. I was sure of it. Just yesterday, I had sat right where those file cabinets were.

My instinct was to head straight to White's office, but then I remembered I had already tried that. I wrote a note for White to contact me and slipped it under his door. *Trust no one, Abby.*

I left the precinct tired and confused. The sun had already started to rise, and it felt comforting against my skin. It was one of the few times I appreciated the temperature.

Not sure of what to do next, I settled on watching a homeless man shuffle along the sidewalk until he disappeared into an alleyway. *What am I still doing here? My investigation is over. I should have been on a plane heading home yesterday. This was not my fight. Nor was it my problem.* I should've listened to myself that day. I made a lot of sense right then.

I'm sure whoever sent Stevie Roscoe after me knew he was dead and could possibly come after me again. That's not usually something I would shy away from, except the situation at home was different. I had two kids and a mother-in-law counting on my return.

I flagged a passing taxi and jumped into the back seat. I had a decision to make. I could either get the hell out of town or head straight toward the beast.

90

The cab screeched to a stop at 9240 Dwight Street. I handed the driver thirty bucks and stepped out. I followed the long oval driveway that led to a Spanish colonial-style mansion. I looked at my watch; it was nearing 7:00 a.m. *He should be home.*

I had not personally met the mayor of Detroit, but I had seen his picture hanging in the precinct. He looked rather charismatic, if I were to judge him by his picture alone. But I knew that wasn't the case. He had a tight grip on that city, and no one made a move without him knowing about it. Time to find out if the mayor set Stevie Roscoe loose on me.

The house appeared quiet. I wondered about his family and whether he had kids. If he did, they would be up by now.

Instead of knocking on the large double oak doors, I stepped off to the side from the front entrance and peeked through a window. I wasn't taking any chances.

If he had anything to do with sending Stevie after me, I could bet he hadn't changed his mind. As far as I was concerned, I was on my own out here. It would be very easy to make me disappear.

No signs of life so far. I removed my weapon and chambered a round. So I was on edge. Who wouldn't be?

I moved around to the left side of the house and peeked through the windows lining the mansion—still no movement inside. I listened for a moment. My phone beeped, causing me to suck a breath in. *Chill, Abby.*

It was Ryan texting me. *Strange, it's 4:30 in the morning at home.* He wanted permission for a sleepover. I noticed the time. The text was sent yesterday. *Shit!* Every now and then I got a text a day late. I could hear it now: *"You always answer Lucy's texts and not mine."* The one time he texts me while I'm away, my phone screws me. I flipped the phone to vibrate mode, pocketed it, and forged ahead.

A wrought-iron gate blocked the path. It wasn't locked, so I proceeded until I reached the back of the property. There was a garden and more pathways leading to a pool. Beyond that was the Detroit River.

I stuck close to the walls of the mansion, doing my best to look invisible. It seemed odd that I had gotten that far on the mayor's property without alerting anyone. There were no visual signs of guards, and I didn't get the impression I had tripped any alarms, but my gut had started to churn, a sure sign things weren't right.

I stopped just short of the floor-to-ceiling windows lining the outdoor patio. About twenty feet from me were French doors leading inside. I listened for a moment before taking a peek. Again, the house appeared empty. I was starting to think no one was home.

I stood up for a better look. That time, I planted my face against the window and used my hand to help diminish the glare on the glass. The patio led straight into a large open kitchen. I didn't see signs that breakfast had been prepared or eaten. *Maybe he's out of town? His alibi?* I found myself asking the same question again: *do I stick around or do I get the hell out of here?*

The hand that grabbed my hair and yanked me back gave me my answer.

91

The first thing I became aware of when I opened my eyes was that I hurt. My face, mostly. My left cheek throbbed, and my mouth tasted metallic. I tried to recall what had happened, but it all took place so fast. The second thing that grabbed my attention was a tightly wound rope cutting into my arms. I was tied to a wooden chair, and my shoes were missing.

I looked around as best I could. The structure was fairly small, maybe eight feet by twelve feet. Gardening tools hung along one wall, and lawn-maintenance equipment lined the other side. There were bags stacked high behind me—fertilizer most likely. I figured I was in the shed I had seen earlier in the garden. The only source of light was a small window. It was filthy. I doubted anyone could see me inside while passing.

Time was not on my side. I knew I had to get out of there. Whoever tied me up had plans to come back. I worked to free my hands, but duct tape had them secured tightly behind the chair. A dull pain was noticeable in both of my shoulders. It felt like any sudden movement might pop them out of their sockets.

I wasn't sure how long I had been unconscious, but

gauging from the temperature in the shack, it couldn't have been long. If the temperature outside had increased to triple digits, I would have literally baked alive inside that tin oven. *Maybe that's the plan?*

• • •

A slap to the face woke me up again. The heat reminded me of where I was. My tongue was sticky, and my throat was scratchy. Sweat seemed to be leaking from every pore on my body. My jeans and blouse both clung to me like thirsty sponges. I no longer had any feeling in my shoulders and part of my arm.

Another slap to the face got me to focus on the man sitting in front of me.

"It was you," was all I could manage.

A smile grew across Leon Briggs' face before he slapped me once more. He enjoyed slapping me. That last one had him giggling.

"Why?" I asked.

"Why? Bitch, you know why. You brought this upon yourself. Investigating shit you're not supposed to be investigating. That's your downfall. You think it's what makes you good at what you do. Uh-huh."

"I get it," I said. I lifted my head so I could look at him. "I could have gone home after capturing the Carters, but I didn't. I was told to forget about Blade Garrison, but I didn't. I had numerous warnings, and I ignored them all. But that's not my downfall. No, that's exactly how I solve crimes. I investigate everything."

Briggs leaned in. His eyes were dark and held steady on me. Sweat snaked its way along the sides of his face. "You must have been a nosy kid growing up, always in everyone's business. I bet you weren't liked much. Still aren't, right? Yeah, I know the type." He took a handkerchief out from his pocket and wiped his forehead, then folded it back up neatly. And then he slapped me again.

I couldn't help but chuckle after that one.

"What's so funny?" he asked.

"I was going to say you slap like a bitch, but then it dawned on me that I know a bitch, and she slaps harder than you."

I must have been hit really hard after that, because I don't remember anything but him waking me up again. That time, I decided I would do the talking. "I know about the Carters. When you found out about them from the surveillance team, you opted to put them into your own version of a witness protection program. You used them, like they worked for you. That was the deal in exchange for their freedom, right? Then you set them loose on the street people."

"Genius isn't it?" Briggs said as he relaxed his posture a bit and let his ego show. "That's what I call being creative with the situation. Now people love coming to downtown Detroit. It's vibrant. Restaurants have reopened. It doesn't smell like piss. What's not to like?"

I spit to drain my mouth. "You didn't cut a deal with them to clean up the city. That was a byproduct. You wanted them for something else, an ace in your back pocket."

Even though he still had a grin on his face, I knew he had understood what I had said. And he wasn't denying any of it.

"You used them to kill the RRs. That was your plan all along, wasn't it? You realized Katherine wanted revenge for her father, but she really didn't know who the RRs were, did she? You filled her in. You told her everything she needed to know. That's why she didn't try to go after them sooner."

We stared at each other, neither saying a word. Briggs wasn't about to confirm any of what I had just said.

"You have a wild imagination, Agent," he finally said.

"Why did you suddenly want them dead?" I asked.

Briggs didn't respond. He didn't blink. He didn't move. He only smiled.

Why? I asked myself again. But then I realized it wasn't about the why; it was about the how.

"I'm sorry. I just realized I've been asking you the wrong questions, Mr. Mayor."

He shifted in his seat, but I'd like to think he squirmed.

"Only the right question can yield the right answer. You see, it's not so much *why* would you kill them. It's more about how—*how* did you *know* they *existed*?"

The politician continued to fidget like a little boy caught in a lie. I asked him once again, articulating each word. "How. Did. You. Know?"

For the first time, I watched his smile diminish in size. Hardin had been right all along.

"I don't know what you're talking about," he said.

It was my turn to grin and chuckle. It all made perfect sense.

Briggs was the sixth RR.

92

"You're one of the RRs."

Briggs sat there unresponsive, so I continued.

"You were the silent one. Only Dennis Walters knew about you."

Briggs swallowed. I had him feeling uncomfortable. The tiny rippling that appeared near the rear of his clenched jaw confirmed my suspicions. "What's your connection to Walters? The group was tight, and they all worked at GM. Don't take this personally, but you don't seem like GM material."

Finally, Briggs spoke. "I worked for the union."

"Now it makes sense. You helped ease the closings on your side of the fence and in return… what did you get? Money? Favors you could call in down the line? The RRs all went on to be successful in the auto industry. It would be advantageous for the mayor to be friendly with them, right? That is, until one of them gets a conscience. Is that what happened? Did Dennis Walters start to feel guilty in his old age? Were you worried he might spill the beans, write a tell-all memoir? Huh? Should I speak slower?"

I knew mouthing off wasn't helping me out of that situation, but it sure felt good. I wished I would have had a plan, but I hadn't made much progress with loosening my hands.

"You're a lot smarter than I thought, Agent," Briggs said, surprisingly calm.

"Your plan all along was to get rid of the Carters once the RRs were out of the picture, wasn't it? That's why I was brought in. You knew I would catch them. But *why* did you get rid of all the files on the hostages? Why cover up that information?"

"If you had that knowledge, you would have caught them a lot sooner than I would have liked, Agent."

"So you gave the Carters just enough room to do the job, but not too much that I wouldn't catch them. That's a tough formula to figure out."

The mayor laughed. "Please, I had a contingency plan in place in the event you turned out to be too dumb. But I knew you would solve it."

"And in the end, the Carters would either end up dead or end up in prison for life. The best-case scenario."

"It's the perfect plan, isn't it?" Briggs' smile got wider and his chuckling grew into contained laughter.

I couldn't believe it. I was a pawn who, like everyone else, did the bidding of the mayor. *Now what? Was there more to his plan?*

I wasn't sure if I imagined it or not, but after a few more seconds, I recognized a siren, and it was getting closer. My luck had changed. The funny thing though—

Briggs was still relishing in his success and hadn't stopped patting himself on the back for a job well done.

"That siren isn't for me, is it?" I asked.

"Oh no, no, no. You see, there's been a breach at the property of the mayor's residence. Some nut was seen walking around with a gun." Briggs put on a pair of leather gloves that he removed from the front pocket of the jacket he had on. He then reached behind him and removed my weapon from the back of his pants. He placed it on the shelf next to him. He then removed a second handgun from his pants.

"I feared for my life," he continued, "so I locked and loaded my personal firearm, allowed me by the Second Amendment of the Constitution of the United States, for my protection."

Briggs pulled the slide back on his Glock and chambered a round.

"I saw someone run into the shed. I was positive they had a gun."

Briggs stood up and opened the door to the shed. He then picked up my gun and fired two rounds at the house before returning it to the shelf.

"I went outside to investigate. That's when I saw the intruder in the shed firing at me."

Briggs started walking backward.

"I feared for my life," he said. "I had no choice. I had to defend myself."

He raised his gun and took aim at me. A beat later, he fired.

93

I opened my eyes and saw Briggs lying face down on the lawn. Lieutenant White stood behind him, holding his gun with rigid arms. It took a few seconds for me to realize that Briggs had not fired his gun.

White had yet to move from his firing position. His eyes were locked onto Briggs, looking for any sort of movement. Neither one of us said anything. I drew a sharp breath, unaware of how long I had been holding it—enough to grab White's attention as he looked at me. He slowly lowered his weapon. Seconds later, he untied my hands.

"He had it all set up," I said, squinting. "There was a break-in."

"I know. I got your note right around the time I got a call from him."

White cut the last of the tape, freeing my hands. My shoulders felt better immediately. I looked at him. "You were in on this."

"Sort of. Normally Stevie Roscoe would have arranged for the officers to come out, but that wasn't going to happen. Lucky for you, Briggs called me."

"Why did you shoot him?"

"I couldn't let him kill you. He had taken enough

innocent lives in this town. It had to stop. The time had come to chop the head off the snake. If I didn't do it," White motioned around with his hand, "this would all continue, and I don't think I could have taken it anymore."

I looked at the mayor's body. "What now?"

"This is an easy clean-up," White said with a smile. "A call from the mayor's residence came in a little after 9:00 a.m. An intruder had entered the premises. Officers were dispatched but arrived too late. It's unfortunate, but the mayor was found shot to death." White handed me back my weapon. "He has no friends, you know? Everyone will eagerly go along with what happened."

"But your gun... it was—"

White waved his hand. "It's not my gun. Don't worry about the details, Agent."

I stood up and walked out of the shed, shielding my eyes from the morning sun. I walked over to where Briggs lay—glad he was face down. I looked back at White. "He was the sixth RR, you know."

White put his hands up. "The less I know, the better. I just want to focus on things getting back to normal. I got a wedding coming."

I remembered trying to smile, but I had felt conflicted. Yet another cover-up in the making, and I had taken part in it. Was that what it had come to? I had always done what was right. Going along with White's plan, that wasn't who I was. Yet for some reason, it didn't bother me like I imagined it would. It could have been because that dead bastard on the ground tried to kill me, twice.

"Don't overthink it," White said as he walked over to where I stood. "You did good. Sometimes justice presents itself in strange ways."

Was justice served? Was that truly the end? Even though we had cut off the head, there was no guarantee another wouldn't grow in its place.

But that wasn't my problem. It was Detroit's.

94

As much as I didn't want to, White convinced me to spend a day in the hospital for observation instead of heading home. True to his words, no one came to question me about what had happened at the mayor's residence. I had been filtered out of the situation.

I lay in bed and watched the media report of the murder of Mayor Briggs, just the way White said it would go down. The sentiment—a terrible incident and Mayor Briggs would be missed.

As for Stevie, well, it was reported that he'd been missing for a few days. Don't ask me how they covered up his body at the hotel. I'm sure my rape kit no longer exists.

As far as the general public knew, Mayor Briggs discovered his chief of staff had a drug problem and planned on firing him before he disappeared. That, of course, led Metro Detroit Police to investigate Stevie's disappearance and his possible connection with the Mayor's death. It looked like Stevie Roscoe would take the fall.

When I first arrived in Detroit and discovered Garrison might have been framed, I never would have suspected what my investigation would uncover. How could so many people entrusted with upholding the law disregard their duties and the oath they had taken? The irony was, I had found myself in the same position. And yet somehow, in my head I had justified it. I knew it was wrong, but in return, we had gotten rid of a larger, more dangerous type of wrong. Right?

• • •

Not once had I thought about Detroit after leaving. I didn't miss the Coney Islands or the urban decay. I was happy to put that case behind me. I had almost gotten away with it until Lieutenant White sent me an email. He had attached a picture of his daughter at her wedding. She looked beautiful, and the reception looked expensive; good thing he had a job. He mentioned he had two more months until retirement. I wrote him back and congratulated him. He deserved it.

I was back to normal hours and able to spend time with Ryan and Lucy. Every weekend, the kids and I, and sometimes Po Po, would explore a nearby neighborhood or a city. Sometimes, we would spend the entire day there, and sometimes only a few hours. We had one rule; we had to pick a different location each time until we saw all of the Bay Area.

Last weekend we rode BART across the bay and trounced around the city of Berkeley. We shopped on 4th Street, had lunch at Cheeseboard Pizza, got ice cream at the Ici Ice Cream shop, and much more.

Of course, being in Berkeley reminded me of

Wilkinson, but I didn't dwell on it. I thought that was a good thing. It meant I was moving on. I didn't want to live in the past and be sad. I had given enough to those emotions. And to be honest, my kids brought me so much happiness, there was no way I could be sad. They kept me looking forward instead of back. And I was grateful for that.

Po Po continued to passive-aggressively fight me for mothering duties, but my mom skills had improved greatly; soon I would have the edge. Just yesterday, I had returned from my run early and beat her to breakfast. The kids had eggs that day. Hooray.

As far as I could tell, I was on pace again to beat her to breakfast. I was wrapping up another morning run and approaching my favorite part on Stockton Avenue, right by Washington Square. It was there that three dogs always slept stretched out across the sidewalk. The city had turned a blind eye to them since they were so loved by the neighborhood. Their names were Salametti, Finocchiona and Sopressata, or Sala, Fino and Sata for short.

The three dogs spent most of their time outside of Fanelli's Deli. They really belonged to Mr. Marziello, the owner of the deli. Regardless, everyone helped take care of the animals. People would even sign up on a list to walk them. I liked the dogs for one other reason; at my height, they were often perfectly spaced apart that I could relive my days of track and field. I ran the 110-meter hurdles.

When I approached my first sleeping hurdle, usually it

was Sala, I pretended I had heard the crack of the starting gun and flew out of the starting block.

My left leg shot straight out while my right leg lifted up and out to a horizontal position, bent at the knee. My right arm reached ahead while my left arm pulled itself back. I had perfect form. Years of training had resurfaced and taken over. Three strides—hurdle. Three strides—hurdle. When I sailed over Fino, my favorite of the three, I smiled and thought to myself:

You still got it, Abby.

Get the first three novels from Hutchinson's best selling series. Readers have described it as Tarantino meets The Office with a splash of romance.

The Novels of Ty Hutchinson

Sei Assassin Thrillers

Contract: Snatch

Contract: Sicko

Contract: Primo

Contract: Wolf Den

Contract: Endgame

Abby Kane Thrillers

Corktown

Tenderloin

Russian Hill (CC Trilogy #1)

Lumpini Park (CC Trilogy #2)

Coit Tower (CC Trilogy #3)

Kowloon Bay

Suitcase Girl (SG Trilogy #1)

The Curator (SG Trilogy #2)

Darby Stansfield Thrillers

Chop Suey

Stroganov

Loco Moco

Other Books

The Perfect Plan

The St. Petersburg Confessions

A Note From The Author

Thanks for reading CORKTOWN. If you liked the book, tell your friends and family about it. Tweet it. Update your Facebook status. Blog about it. Give it a shining review. I would genuinely appreciate your kind words.

If for some reason something in the book rubbed you the wrong way, or you have questions about it, email me. I'd love to hear your feedback. I can be reached at thutchinson@me.com.

I tend to hang out in these places.
Blog: http://tyhutchinson.wordpress.com/
Facebook: http://www.facebook.com/tyhutchinson.author

Printed in Great Britain
by Amazon